I0755751

THE MOON IN DEEP WINTER

The Moon in Deep Winter

LEE POLEVOI

Casagrande Press • San Diego, California

Published by Casagrande Press
San Diego, California

www.casagrandepress.com
casagrandepress@aol.com

Book Design: Steve Connell / Transgraphic Services

Printed in the USA

Library of Congress Cataloguing-in-Publication Data

Polevoi, Lee
The moon in deep winter / Lee Polevoi.
p. cm.
ISBN 978-0-9769516-5-0
1. Family—Fiction. 2. Murder—Fiction. 3. New England—Fiction. 4. Domestic fiction. I. Title.

PS3616.O558M66 2008
813'.6—dc22

2008033446

To my mother and father
and to
Maxine

1

FAMILY SECRETS

1

The bus arrived in Rockbridge at six a.m. During the night the temperature had dropped below freezing, and barely moved since. Cold pierced the leaky bus and passengers' clothing. Parker tried ignoring it. He was near the end of a long journey, thousands of miles across the continent, with no trouble to speak of along the way. But as he stepped off the bus by the Rockbridge P.O. and walked through his hometown (pop. 1324) in a sleepless daze, he became aware of a slow-moving patrol car on the gravel road behind him. It was Sunday morning, mid-November, in a year of failed attempts to murder a president and a pope. Gripping his satchel, Parker walked a little faster, in spite of the fact that he was guilty—so far as he knew—of no crime.

Brisk winds swept down Main Street, a bleak processional of small-town businesses, bank and barbershop, Army-Navy store with military surplus gas masks in the display window. Above the town's only major intersection, a stoplight swayed, rusty and defunct. A Sunoco station with a sign CLOSED TIL FERTHER NOTICE pasted on the pump. To the west, the Berkshires rose like blue-gray curls of smoke.

Tires crunched on gravel. Not hard seeing himself through the eyes of the law: male, white, six feet tall, mid- to late-twenties. He heard the tires stop, but the eyewitness description went on in his head. Dark hair, scraggly beard, windbreaker and jeans. Stooped over now against the chilling wind. No visible means of support.

A car door opened. Footsteps thudded in snow behind him. "Hey, hold on there a minute . . ."

He turned to face a short man in a khaki uniform, with skeptical features and mud-colored hair under his cap. A weathered face, someone good at what he does, loyal to the town. Not to be messed with.

"Pardon my asking—you live around here or just passing through?"

He spoke in the broad flattened pitch common to the region. Parker hadn't heard these inflections in a long time. Staring at the badge on his shirt embossed with FRANKLIN COUNTY SHERIFF'S OFFICE, he pictured hand-cuffs, strip search, photos and prints; but it was a good question and deserved an answer.

"Little of both," he said.

The sheriff frowned, pointing at the satchel. "What's in there?"

"Clothes."

"Any liquor?"

"No."

"Narcotics? Firearms?"

"Just clothes," Parker said.

They stood on the curb without speaking. Then the sheriff tilted his head in the direction of the cruiser. "Get in."

"What?" Parker couldn't believe it. "What the hell for?"

"Do yourself a favor," the sheriff said, opening the rear door. "Get in."

The dashboard was cluttered with law enforcement gear—night-stick, walkie-talkie, rifle encased in a leather grip. He wanted to tell the sheriff that he'd crossed a great distance to be here this morning, only after considerable reflection and always with the aching sense that it was a really bad idea. A week ago, drunk and possibly poisoned in a wine cellar in Southern California, coming home seemed like exactly the right thing to do; even the girl in the green-spangled evening dress straddling him at the time agreed. Now he stood ankle-deep in snow with a hostile officer of the law and began having second thoughts.

The sheriff turned from behind the wheel with a strange, lumpy grin. "I'll be damned . . . Parker Sloane, is that you?"

It took a moment to puzzle this out. A name slowly came to mind. "Alf? Alf Cooper?"

The sheriff grinned and nodded. He was an old family acquaintance, a truck farmer who'd once roamed the Massachusetts Turnpike with week-old produce for sale. "Here I am about to run you in for loitering and et cetera." He laughed in a high, thin voice, all suspicion gone. "Back in town, are you? What's the occasion?"

"Seemed like a good idea," he said, much relieved. "So how long have you been sheriff?"

"Ha! Not me. I'm just a deputy. Mostly scribble parking tickets, clean up after the bums heave their guts out in the drunk tank. Tell you one thing, though. Sure beats hell outa hauling cherry tomatoes up and down the goddamn state."

"Well," Parker said, tugging his jacket closer. "That's great."

"Home'd be where you're going, right? Bet you wouldn't mind a ride courtesy of the taxpayers of Franklin County."

Fortunately, rather than a barrage of personal questions on the way home, Alf Cooper relaxed into silence. They drove through stretches of woods and open farmland. Sunlight glinted on snow, poplars nearest the road bent over with ice. In summer, he remembered, rows of green tobacco leaves rippled in the breeze.

OK, he thought, a *little* trouble.

The trip east had taken five days across snowy interstates, past truck stops and fierce desert sunsets, the ghostly lights of distant mountain cities. In a diner outside Reno he fell into conversation with a bristle-haired cattle feed salesman over the relative depth and quality of the Broncos' secondary versus that of his own New England Patriots. He had no strong feelings on the matter one way or another, but the feed salesman's belligerently-expressed convictions fueled a sudden rage in him, coming on like an episode of *petit mal*. The next thing he knew his slice of pecan pie a la mode was dripping down the other guy's face, arms and legs and bodies getting between them, breaking it up. In the end, no more than pride was hurt—apologies made, all the passengers returned to the bus—the only lingering question being, would he be allowed back on, too? A convincing show of contrition on his part, plus his last fifty dollars, persuaded the bus driver to overlook the whole squalid event. The feed salesman got off in Omaha. For the rest of the long journey, Parker kept quiet.

In the hills of Vermont, the bus stopped at a railroad crossing alongside a farmer in a compact tractor and waited for the Central Maine freight train to rumble by. From his warm seat on the bus, Parker watched snow fall on the front-end loader and the driver's John Deere cap. He shivered in sympathy. Any number of things could explain the pecan pie outburst. Looking down on the snow-covered farmer, Parker thought, I just need some time out, is all.

Alf Cooper was humming to himself as they came to the bottom of a steep hill, the last before the family house. Parker asked to be dropped off.

"But we just got this one last hill—"

"Thanks. I don't mind walking."

Alf pulled over and parked by the side of the road, but at first Parker didn't move. Time was running out, precious seconds left in which to change his mind and keep on going, disappearing into Newfoundland perhaps, or adrift in the Arctic Sea. Not pleasant to contemplate, but at the moment not altogether out of the question. And it was now that Alf decided to get personal.

"So where you been? What you been up to?"

"California," he said, as an answer to both.

"Nothing like this, I bet." He gestured at the snowbound landscape. "Snow's been coming down hard since middle of last week. Gets worse every year, I think."

Still Parker didn't move, wondering if for some reason Alf

wanted to greet the family, too. It didn't seem right to be handing out invitations, but he felt obliged to say something.

"Do you uh want to come to the house?"

The deputy sheriff's eyes widened, as if he'd stepped on a nail. "No," he said.

"Well then . . ."

Getting out of the car he heard Alf grumble to himself over the crackling radio. "Come in? I sure as hell do not." He swung the cruiser around sharply, sending Parker scrambling for safety, and headed back to Rockbridge.

Even in sunlight, the air was bitterly cold. At the top of the hill, fields extended to wooded countryside a half-acre away. Closer in, the two-story Colonial house—slate roof, pine-bright timber—was bordered by a low stone wall. In the front yard, the same towering rock elm. Nothing else for miles around, all as he remembered it.

On the porch he blew warm air in his cupped hands and knocked on the thick oak door, ransacking his brain for memories of his mother and stepfather happy and in love, children rushing up and down the stairs, Burke's elderly mother asleep in the rocker. He knocked again, remorse bubbling up in his chest. Eugenia was surely long since dead.

He tried the door. Open. Sunlight swept in, dancing on air.

"Hello? Anybody home?"

In the living room there was the familiar covered sofa and polished-glass end tables. A row of daguerreotypes on the mantel above the fireplace. *Home.* He felt giddy with déjà vu, like too much oxygen on the brain.

A scraping sound echoed from somewhere in the house. He looked down the hallway. "Mother? Is that you?"

The kitchen was different, repainted, from bilge-gray walls to a light summery blue. A mahogany breakfast table he'd never seen before. But the kitchen felt long-uninhabited, as if a vast silence descended from the attic and second-floor bedrooms down to the clean blue space he was standing in now. A mausoleum silence—like death, he thought. Bright shiny death.

"Walt? Rita?"

More than five years had passed since he'd been in this house. Anything could have happened during that time. What if they'd moved out and Alf Cooper forgot to mention it? What if the furniture and appliances belong to strangers, a family of strangers?

There was that scraping sound again, a distinct squeak of metal scratching wood. He followed it into the den, where a weak light suffused the tall windows, falling on ceiling beams and the pea-green surface of a pool table in the center of the room. In the corner, the source of the abrasive noise: Eugenia Pratt Sullivan, a small woman in a black shawl and gingham dress, seated in the rocker and dragging a steel-tipped walking cane across the hardwood floor. Parker, leaning over to investigate, saw the cane nudging a hunk of aged mozzarella toward a wary, yet fascinated, field mouse.

"Come and get it, Mister Mouse," the old woman said in a dry Back Bay voice. "Come get this nice piece of cheese."

The mouse, a hungry-looking stray from the woods out back, cast a skittish glance up at Parker—friend or foe?—while Eugenia lifted the cane as far up in the air as her arthritic limbs allowed.

"Just a little closer . . ."

He remembered timeless afternoons of his childhood, planted on her lap listening to tales of witch trials and capsized whaling boats. Happy and relieved by her ongoing presence, he cried out, "Eugenia! Look who's here!" At the sound of his voice, she twitched in the rocker. The cane struck empty floor; gone, with cheese, was the field mouse.

"It's me." He came over and hugged her, smelling lilac and wrinkled flesh. "Parker."

She blinked at the floor. "Parker?" she said, as if addressing the vanished field mouse. His name sounded odd and foreign when she said it, even to him. Kneeling, he took hold of her hands—cool, vulnerable, like pressing dead leaves—and squeezed. First he had to get her attention.

"Yes, remember me? I've been away for awhile."

"Of course I remember." Eugenia wore a hearing aid and talked loudly. "You live around here, don't you?"

"No, but I used to. I used to live right here."

How old was she now? Eighty, eight-five? There was still a sneak thief's wicked glint in her eye.

"You're the one who set fire to the saltbox house," she declared. "As I recall, the entire estate went up in smoke." She sighed, patting her thin white hair in place and tugging the shawl close. "Things were never the same after that."

He gripped her hands, suddenly desperate to be recognized.

"Remember when I was little? We used to catch fireflies outside and bring them in to show you. What about the time

I came to the table with a bullfrog and it hopped in the salad bowl and the cranberry sauce?" He paused, a lump of ungainly proportions lodged in his throat. "Remember?"

Eugenia appeared to smile, fragmentary molars dotting her open mouth. "Fireflies? Cranberry sauce?"

"That's right."

"Come here to me."

Folded in her skeletal embrace, Parker felt certain at last that he'd done the right thing coming home. This house, this family. It felt good to be back.

From the hall came sounds of arrival—a dog's bark, the front door opening, wet boots crunching on the floor. He thought: I know that bark. A deep voice thundered down the hall like rolling artillery fire.

"Hey! Where is everybody?"

Burke. Another wave of joy washed over him. This was going much better than expected, seeing family members one at a time, instead of the chaos of everyone at once. As he turned to the doorway, he felt clear-headed and pure of heart, for the first time in many years. Eugenia knows me. The rest is easy.

Behind his back, however, the object of his inspiration let out a deafening howl.

"Burke, come quick! I need you!"

Turning again, he narrowly avoided the cane as it splintered the lip of the pool table. He grabbed her frail shoulders to calm her, but this only prompted a longer, tooth-grinding scream.

"Help! Help! He's starting another fire!"

From the hall, the booming artillery voice. "What the hell

is going on?"

He saw Ajax first, a chocolate Lab retriever grown old and white around the muzzle. Then his stepfather in brush pants, hip boots and plaid hunting vest. A Remington twelve-gauge shotgun at his side. There were new wrinkles in his face, and his head was completely bald now, but he appeared as tall and thick-muscled as ever. Peering through the den's shadows at the bearded intruder poised above his dear old mother.

"Well . . ." Parker grinned foolishly. "I bet this is a surprise."

"Look out! He's got matches!"

Time abruptly slowed down, or it seemed like that in his muddled perceptions. It seemed to take Burke forever to raise the shotgun and aim eye-level with him across the den. Parker stared, unable to move, less from fear than from disbelief.

"Wait a minute," he said.

"Hurry!" Eugenia cried. "Save the estate!" And delivered a pre-emptive strike with the cane, a stinging blow to the base of his spine that sent him reeling against the pool table. There was a flash of light and sound. He thudded head-first onto the floor, as inches from his face the window exploded, showering him with plaster-and-glass confetti.

A long time passed before he realized: I'm not dead. Ajax snarled at him through the legs of the pool table, and footsteps were coming closer—the sound he imagined death might make stopping you on the street, tapping your shoulder to say, *Today's your lucky day*. Still he knew it was better being upright, for whatever came next.

He stood, took in an overwhelming smell of dust and gunpowder residue. The ceiling wobbled. Something hard and warm pressed in his chest. He looked down at the steel barrels, then up into Burke's florid face. He said his name; he could hear himself saying it; nothing came out.

Now, at the point of death, Parker felt wronged and offended. This wasn't the homecoming he'd expected, the grand family dinner and afterward sitting by the fire, catching up on old times. He closed his eyes, heard the seductive click of the trigger. Now there would be no family dinner, no nights with bullfrogs and shooting stars.

"You know," he heard a timid voice say, "that's not the one with the matches, that's, that's . . ."

He opened his eyes as Burke's face creased with recognition, giving way to a reluctant smile. The killing edge still lit his cool blue eyes—shaded now, Parker could see, by a trace of disappointment.

"Welcome home, son."

2

Years ago, Burke scorned all worldly ambitions, denouncing civilized life beyond the house—"out there," as he put it. I've been out there, he'd say, stationed at dismal backwater posts from New Delhi to Bogotá. I've seen famine, insurrection, epidemic disease. It's a shithole, son, contaminates everyone who goes near it. Parker, just turned eighteen and headed for college, heard instead: *If you leave now, you leave for good.* He'd responded heatedly to this unspoken challenge and yet another fight had broken out between them.

The gunshot blast still rang in the den. Wind swept through what was left of the window. He touched his face and felt blood.

Probably Burke recognized him right off, and what happened after that had nothing to do with mistaken identity. Same tactics as before. Rattle your opponent, seize the upper hand. Gamesmanship.

But worse even than being shot at, in his mind, was the

sorry spectacle he'd made cowering beneath the pool table, a demented old woman and trigger-happy stepfather witness to his humiliation. For that, and for the rancid taste fear had left in his mouth, he wished to thrash them both to within an inch of their lives with the steel-tipped walking cane.

No denying it; he was badly rattled.

A short time later Burke returned. He'd changed into brown corduroys and a coiled white Norwegian sweater. Strolling across the den and opening the liquor cabinet, he resembled nothing so much as a game warden in his golden years.

"Didn't get around to tidying up, I see."

"Send me the bill."

Burke laughed. "Forget it. Let's have a drink."

Shouldn't there be an apology for his actions, some acknowledgement that the great white hunter had fired in error? But there was nothing remorseful in the way Burke uncorked a decanter and poured its contents into two glasses.

"I recommend the house brandy—"

An admission of guilt, a hint of personal responsibility?

"A modest, yet ingratiating Napoleon . . ."

Parker walked over and stood face-to-face with him, the air between them as cramped and testy as just a half-hour ago—except this time no twelve-gauge was pressed into his chest.

"You knew, didn't you?"

Burke shrugged.

"Damn it! You almost killed me!"

"Look at it from my perspective," his stepfather said, handing him a glass. "I walk in from a morning of bad hunting and what do I find but a wild-eyed drifter terrorizing my ninety-six-year-old mother—in my own home! Seems to me I had the God-given right to shoot you dead in your tracks."

Parker was confused. "She's not that old, is she?"

"Ha! Then you admit it."

There was the muted sound of tires on gravel. A battered green pickup rolled past where the window had been. Moments later, he heard the back door open and different sets of boots stomp dry on the welcome mat in the kitchen. His outrage melted away to a tingly anticipation.

First in the doorway was Walt, a broad-shouldered young man in grease-stained overalls, two years younger than Parker, grown tall and chunky like his old man. Thick, uncombed straw-colored hair. Squinting into the den through wire-rim glasses.

"I smell smoke."

"That's because," Burke said, "your brother nearly got his tail shot off for breaking and entering."

Walt went blank, as if he'd been asked directions to Mars. "Brother?"

"Hi," Parker said.

Without prompting from anyone, Burke launched into a colorful account of Parker's homecoming, up to and including a dramatic chase into the woods, the two of them wrestling for possession of the shotgun until Burke laid him out with a mighty left hook.

"That's all behind us now. Forgive and forget, I always say."

Parker smiled. *Gamesmanship*. Maybe because he was older now, he could see the humor in it. "That's the movie version," he told Walt. "It was just a little misunderstanding. Anyway, here

I am."

"Why?" Walt asked.

"Why what?"

"Why are you here? Where'd you come from? What do you want?"

"Slow down," Parker said. "I just got here."

Burke eased into the leather armchair. "Give the boy some breathing space. He'll fill us in when he's good and ready, won't you, son?"

" . . . Sure."

"There, you see? We have his word on it."

Mother appeared in galoshes and a drab winter coat. Her brown hair was flecked with gray, and she was smaller and heavier than he remembered. One look at him and she dropped her purse. "I don't believe it." He glanced at Burke—*she* had no problem recognizing me!—and then Mother swept him up in a fervent embrace. Over the top of her head he saw Rita in the doorway, a slender pale-eyed girl with black hair falling to her shoulders. Hanging back, hands deep inside her coat pockets, watching intently. Twenty-two years old, he calculated, and very different from the gangly teenager who used to live here. He gazed at her, at all of them, across a great expanse of time and space. Too happy to speak.

In the bathroom mirror he examined his wounds. Tiny scars were etched in his cheekbones, but no glass had sunk into flesh. Something's wrong here, he thought, something awkward and weird and out of place. "Me," he told the face in the mirror, with its long hair and hardscrabble beard, skin weathered by too many days in the sun. A kind face, but only if you know me.

On the long bus ride home he dreamed several times about his father—not the way he was, but a composite gleaned from years of hearsay and evidence Mother grudgingly offered up. His father's shoe size and favorite color, the way his left elbow hung funny after a badly healed stress fracture. But the facts lacked substance and were subject to change, depending on her mood. All he knew for sure was that his father worked in the Commerce Department during the Eisenhower administration, and that on a belated honeymoon two years into the marriage—baby Parker left behind with relatives in D.C.—he drowned in the swimming pool of a Howard Johnson's Motor Lodge outside Arlington, Virginia.

After the funeral, they resumed their lives in the cramped Bethesda row house. He entered kindergarten, Mother found a clerk-typist job in his father's old office at the Small Business Administration. Many late-night macaroni-and-cheese dinners, Mother falling asleep at the table.

In second grade, everything changed. At the urging of friends, she went out one night to a reception at the Egyptian embassy, where she met a tall, handsome Foreign Service officer named Burke Sullivan. Not long afterward, this person Burke showed up for dinner, swaggering and immense in a charcoal seersucker suit, making a show of shaking Parker's little hand and praising its resolute grip—the ill will between us, he was convinced, dated from that time—and then, too soon to understand, Mother and Burke were married. Other children, Walt and Rita, appeared. And one day out of the blue

Burke announced his retirement from the State Department and relocated the family to this house in the woods, presided over by his mother, a doddering relic of wealth.

Looking back, Parker could vaguely recall the scent of cherry blossoms along a winding river. He had no memories of his father.

"First you were going to be an astronaut," Mother said in the kitchen. "Then it was baseball, you wanted to be one of those players with the funny name—you know, they throw the ball left-handed . . ."

Recent events had soured him on childish aspirations. "Southpaw," he said.

"Yes, that's it."

From the breakfast table he watched Mother move swiftly among appliances in her yellow flowered smock. She diced onions, stripped layers of fat off chicken breasts, slid a three-bean casserole into the oven. Afternoon light seeped like oil across the kitchen floor.

"And one morning you came home from school and announced you were running for President! What ambitions you had."

Ambitions? He could rattle off a dozen lifetime goals, each loftier than the last but in the end fruitless, in pursuit of which in its latest incarnation he'd been left bloody and beaten in a ditch somewhere south of the border, a career move he'd recommend to no one.

"I don't remember ever running for president."

"Well you did!"

Sounds of life pervaded the house: Eugenia shuffling down

the hall, bursts of classical music from the second floor. Outside the window Burke shouting instructions to Ajax, the old dog wagging his tail in the snow and otherwise doing nothing. Sound triggered memories, like a splash of cold water in the face—autumn mornings, kids playing in the rock elm's gold-and-red fallen leaves. He sighed; it was like trying to visualize the law of gravity. Under his breath he muttered, "Shit."

Mother shot him a dark look: no obscenities on Sunday, please. A light thumping on floorboards accompanied the music overhead.

"What's that?"

"Rita."

"What's she doing?"

"Dancing." Mother slipped her hands inside oven mitts and lifted a pot of steaming potatoes off the stove. "And Walt no doubt's locked up in his room, tinkering with that contraption of his. You're in luck," she said, with scarcely hidden sarcasm, "we hardly ever see each other, except at meals."

He looked at salt and pepper shakers on the table, shaped like tiny windmills. *In luck.*

Setting the pot on the edge of the sink, she drained the potatoes inside. Steam clouded her face. "You know, Parker, you could have let us know you were coming. We could have picked you up in Rockbridge, saved you that long walk in the snow."

"I didn't walk. I got a ride."

Mother began grinding the potatoes with a steel masher. "Oh? From whom?"

"Alf Cooper! Remember him?"

"Yes," she said, after a pause, "I do."

"A deputy sheriff! And he knew me right away."

Outside, Burke continued to issue commands, muffled by the window: "Sit! Roll over! Play dead!" Ajax barked and barked, did little else.

"No one's teaching *that* old dog any new tricks," she said.

He watched her mash potatoes at the sink, her graying hair and sagging shoulders. She had wistful green eyes, an Irish shade passed on to Rita. In old photographs she smiled warmly, a pretty corn-fed Ohio girl. Now the double chins and the lines in her face reminded him, everyone grows old. He'd always hoped for exceptions, himself included—but Mother was growing old anyway, no matter what he hoped for.

"Will you please stop staring at me?"

"Sorry."

"Look at you! There used to be some meat on those bones—and all that hair! Who can find you under all that hair?"

He splayed his fingers across the table and thought: I could use a drink. Upstairs, music swelled to a crescendo, with a series of *thumps*! Lightly skating on floorboards over their heads. Rita, dancing.

"Tell me about him."

"Who?"

"My father."

"Your father . . ." She set down the steel utensil, looked out the window at an empty field of snow. He'd revived what she considered a pointless childhood ritual: the plea for facts and Mother's vague, shrugging response. "What's to tell? He stood five foot nine in his stocking feet. He was good with numbers. Veal cutlets made him ill. Every now and then he liked a good polka. And he drowned in the deep end of a Howard Johnson's swimming pool on the eve of our second wedding anniversary."

Facts, yes, but nothing Parker could work with. In the meantime Mother continued to talk, uncharacteristically, about her own earlier life growing up lonely and Catholic in Zanesville, Ohio. At nineteen, she eloped with Parker's father and went to live in the nation's capital with her new Presbyterian husband. Her family, opposed to the marriage from the beginning, never forgave her.

"So naturally when he died, everyone back in Zanesville called it divine judgment. But I still had *you* to take care of, didn't I? I went to work at the SBA and made a good home for you, never went out or saw anybody until one night in 1957 when I met Burke Sullivan—at that time in my tender youth, the most exotic and intriguing man I'd ever met." A dismal smile appeared on her face. "Of course, that was all a long time ago."

"And far, far away," he added.

"The point is, there's never a time when you're truly alone. Someone or something is always at hand. And do you know why?"

Disturbed by this turn in conversation, he picked up the windmill shakers and crashed them together, making small explosive noises.

"Because it's—Parker, stop doing that!—because it's His will."

The capital "H" in her voice was scary enough; she'd never been religious before. "What did you say about Walt's contraption?"

"He's building an airplane. With his bare hands, he says."

Parker laughed. "Where? In his room?"

"I doubt it. But then I doubt most of what he tells me. Of course, he tells me very little to begin with."

"Why?"

"Why? Because he believes his mother is very *stupid*—"

"No," he said urgently, "why is he building an airplane?"

"I really couldn't say!"

Silence, except for a clock ticking on top of the stove and the hiss of residual steam from the sink. "How about Eugenia?" he asked. "She sure looks fit, not a day over—"

"Fit? *Fit?* What's that supposed to mean?"

"Doesn't she?"

At last Mother saw his confusion. Carefully setting bowls on the counter soup-kitchen style, she walked to the breakfast table where he sat and took both his hands in her oven mitts, still holding the oven's warm after-glow.

"Parker, you drop in one morning out of nowhere and expect things haven't changed. Well, they do. You can't ever predict what's going to happen. I couldn't imagine having children again after your father died, and the Good Lord blessed me with two. I never thought I'd see you again and now all of a sudden here you are . . ."

He stood to embrace her, but Mother turned away, preparing to ladle out bowls of clam chowder. "Here," she said, handing him a bowl. "Make yourself useful."

He looked at her.

"You're home now," she said. "Isn't that the most important thing?"

3

Eugenia had been left a small fortune when her husband, Calvin, a prosperous New Bedford ship-owner, succumbed to the influenza epidemic of 1919. Over the years she'd frittered it away, and her life with it; by the time Burke arrived with his family, it was only his government pension that allowed them to live on the fringes of wealth—comfortably, without pretension—and Parker grew up believing they were privileged to own this house in the woods.

Now the dining room's furniture and décor suggested a false bravado, remnants of better days—half polished silverware, orange and purple-spotted wood lilies in a vase with a hairline crack in it. Nothing enhanced or renewed over time.

He had to admit, though, the majesty of food arrayed on the dining room table was impressive. Three-bean salad, simmering roast chicken. Bright green steamed asparagus set beside orange yams. Served with a bottle of red wine.

He sat facing his siblings, Eugenia at his side, Burke in a

maroon smoking jacket at the head of the table. Mother finally finished up in the kitchen and hurried out to take her seat at the opposite end. Folding her hands, she led the family in prayer.

"Lord, for what we're about to receive, we thank you . . ."

Head bowed, he was aware of the dining room's confined dimensions, barely large enough for the antique pedestal table and the chipped china cabinet in the corner. Once upon a time children sat around this table, children who'd expanded with greater density and mass, in effect crowding out their elders. Even now, Eugenia appeared to be visibly shrinking.

"—your everlasting mercy. Amen."

A dizzying commotion followed. Walt grabbed the plate of yams, Burke seized the roast chicken, only Rita waiting out the frenzy. Mother reached for the asparagus just as Eugenia's arthritic hand clamped down the bowl. A struggle ensued; Mother's relative strength and vitality prevailed.

"Today was my best class yet," Rita said brightly. "For the first time I felt like I'm really making progress, that this dance thing isn't a big waste of time." She paused, looking embarrassed. "Maybe no one wants to hear . . ."

"Of course we do, dear," Mother said.

"It's just that sometimes weeks go by without any improvement, I trip all over myself in the middle of an exercise I just want to give up. Today was different. The *glissade* went perfectly, and Mrs. Spoto asked me to demonstrate for the class."

Everyone nodded, their mouths full. Parker was amazed at how hungry he was, at how good a home-cooked meal could be after all this time.

"I hear it's gonna snow again real soon," Walt said.

Mother shivered. "Remember that terrible snowstorm last year? Six feet of snow in twenty-four hours!"

"Like Yugoslavia," Burke said.

She looked at him. "Pardon me?"

"Mountain strongholds. Winter of '44."

Mother groaned, helping herself to the bottle of wine. A short time later Parker sat back from the table and gazed at his family through the eyes of a well-fed stranger: at Walt's pug nose and twitchy eyebrows, Mother's steam-tangled hair. Burke was absorbed in slicing roast chicken into precise, delicate portions.

And Rita, look at how she'd changed. He watched her drink from a water goblet, admiring her long black hair and sea-green eyes, a lithe purposeful dancer's body in jeans and a red leotard top. A drop of water gleamed on her lip like a star. As a child, she'd never been terribly appealing. He couldn't get over the change.

Rita met his eyes and quickly looked away. Maybe she was thinking the same thing about him.

"Eugenia," Mother said, "you haven't touched your clam chowder."

"I don't care for clam chowder. You ought to know that by now."

They exchanged looks. Returning to her plate, Mother speared an asparagus stalk and asked, "So you were saying . . .?"

"Colder than hell," Burke said. "Goddamn partisans couldn't agree on the time of day . . ."

"No," Mother said. "Not you."

A long moment passed before Parker realized *he* was the one being addressed. In fact, they wall seemed to wait on his answer.

"Me? Did I say something?"

"Yeah." Walt's eyes darted like fish behind his thick glasses. "You were gonna tell us what you've been doing all this time."

The wine bottle was on the table in front of him, and he poured a glass. Beyond the French doors, the sky was milky yellow, sign of impending snow. Was he ready for this? He said, "It's kind of a long story."

"So what? We're not going anywhere."

Rita touched Walt's elbow, a scolding gesture. "Don't tease him. That's not nice." Instantly he surrendered, hunched over to consume more yams. When she looked across the table at Parker, he could feel his face burning.

"It's OK," she said. "You don't have to feel pressured."

But he *did* feel pressured, massively so. On the long bus ride home he had plenty of time to concoct alternate versions of his life, from the mundane to the ridiculous and not excluding careers as a stockbroker, lion-tamer, highway patrolman. Now, according to his plan, all he had to do was pick one.

"Son, I'm curious about the luggage."

"What luggage?"

"That's what I mean," Burke said. "You don't seem to have any."

"I travel light."

The family watched and waited. Do I tell the truth or not? Under the table, Ajax was sniffing at his knees. Probably not.

"I've had some luck," he said. "Somehow I've managed to

be in the right place at the right time." He forced a laugh. "A lot can happen in five years, right? Maybe I'll just touch on the highlights, so we're not sitting here all night."

Another glass of wine and imagination took over. He delivered an account of the past five years that intersected with reality from time to time without ever breaking the flow. Careers wide and varied, a bike messenger in Manhattan, undertaker's assistant in South Carolina, various "white-collar gigs" in Houston and New Orleans, and his most recent success with a visionary group of L.A. developers and their latest venture, *Condominios en los Tropicos,* a deluxe resort community to be built in Baja California. Nowhere in this account was there mention of a lanky Frenchman named Jean-Paul, a wheeler and dealer on the fringes of the industry, on whose behalf Parker agreed to smuggle fifty thousand dollars to unnamed associates in Mexico City. And who, feeling betrayed by his apprentice in matters of the heart, arranged to have him beaten and left for dead somewhere south of the Rio Grande. Instead he described lunching with bankers and architects, all-night power sessions in lavish Beverly Hills office suites, even—Who says it's *truth* that sets you free?—ground-breaking ceremonies at the beach in San Felipe, the balmy waters of the Sea of Cortez running through his toes.

He paused, looking over the faces of his loved ones, and thought: I seem to have their attention. Mostly he wanted to impress Rita.

"Lately I've been thinking about coming home, you know? Wondering how all of you were doing. That other stuff doesn't matter. I'm glad I made the trip and I hope we can all forget the past, just move on from here."

And sat back, wearied by his own rhetoric. Eugenia was first to respond, taking a teaspoon and planting it upright on the table. "I remember when you were just *this* high off the ground."

Rita came through. "Amazing," she said. Mother heartily agreed, Walt squinted at him as if he were a shiny toy. Even Burke seemed persuaded.

"Very impressive, son. I expect you had your reasons for not sharing this grand news with us sooner."

He relied now on mental dexterity and intake of wine to get him through. "With projects like this, you have to be discreet. Can't go around broadcasting your intentions in the town square, at least not until everything's signed, sealed and delivered."

"And the rest of it?"

"Rest of what?"

Burke waved at him. "The beard, your appearance overall, would seem to belie this astonishing success story."

"Oh, that." He grinned. "We're pretty casual on the coast."

As the family took this all in, he lingered comfortably inside his new body armor of power and wealth. Mother and Rita were beaming; he figured he'd pulled it off.

Then Burke turned to Walt, a harsh unforgiving expression on his face.

"So what have we learned from this?"

"Huh?"

"'*Huh?*'" The old man's sneering mimicry was dead-on. "We've learned, damn it, that a person can make something of himself, given enough time and ambition. You have to take advantage of your upbringing. Young Parker here is living proof of it."

"But—"

"Have you ever gone hungry? Ever gone without blankets or clothing?" His sudden ire chilled the room. "Haven't you always had everything you wanted?"

Clearly an answer was expected, of Walt and the others as well. Parker was enormously dismayed to have been so convincing.

"*Haven't you?*"

"Yeah," Walt grumbled.

"We sure have," Rita said.

"Me, too!" Eugenia wagged the teaspoon at Parker. "All that what you just said? I don't believe a word of it, not a word. I know for a fact that you lit out for the woods with that Finnish logging crew, just after the Great War."

Logging crew? He smiled at her like a talk-show host. "I never did that, Eugenia."

"You certainly did! Walked out of the house on Beacon Street in the middle of Christmas dinner, didn't show up again until spring of 1923. Lord, the stories you had to tell!" The old woman looked around the table at no one in particular. "You think *this* is cold? Up there it's much, much worse. Loggers spike their tea with kerosene to keep warm. Dip their feet in hot lard just so they can pull their socks on in the morning."

He felt loopy from these so-called facts and memories, at the same time aware of the depth of unease at the table. Meanwhile Walt stood, marched over behind Mother's chair and took hold of her shoulders.

"Thinking about us, huh? How come you didn't write or call or nothing? For all we know you've stole money from this condo thing. Maybe they found out and now you're on the run. Maybe on the FBI Ten Most Wanted—"

"Maybe you should shut the hell up," Parker said.

This got a laugh out of Burke, while Mother collapsed in a coughing fit. No matter how much time had passed, this was no way for the children to talk. "Who wants seconds?" she asked, upon recovering. Rita, who'd hardly touched her food, said, "I do."

The old man continued to regard Walt with scorn. "You're way out of line here, pal."

"He's my brother," Walt said, trying not to whine. "I can say whatever I want."

"Well, what about you?"

"What *about* me?"

"Please," Rita said, "let's have a nice—"

"What have you amounted to? Tell us that. Tell us about all your stellar achievements."

Walt stood frozen with rage behind his mother's chair. Let's not fuss over a little pack of lies, he thought. Before he could intercede, however, Eugenia's stiff fingers handcuffed his wrist.

"I know what it's like up there," she whispered. "Chopping down fifty foot trees in the dead of winter—"

"We're not talking about me," Walt pleaded.

"Eating wood ants for breakfast—"

"We are now!" Burke roared. "What the hell is it you do

besides reading comic books all day?"

"Defecating in the snow—"

"Not comic books! Blueprints!"

"Please," Rita said.

"Crazy Finns running outside, jumping in the sauna—"

"Blueprints?"

"Naked as jaybirds—"

"Is that any kind of rational approach to living in the real—"

He shook free of the old woman's grip and brought his fist down on the table. Glasses clinked, serving bowls rattled.

"Let's have some order here."

Walt limped back to his chair. The others looked at their plates, chastened.

"I'd love to meet a Finn someday," Eugenia said with a sigh. "I think they're so . . . robust."

Parker sighed too, fending off bad feelings about himself. "OK," he said, "things have worked out. Life is good. I make a comfortable living." One last lie; he was broke. "None of that matters. Not compared to having a place to come home to, a place you can say, *Here,* this is where I'm from . . ." A place like this? he thought. With nude Finns and twelve-gauge shotguns? "This is what really matters."

His audience appeared mollified; only Walt's scowl indicated nothing like approval.

"What about your chowder?" Mother said, pushing the bowl at Eugenia. "Have some."

"It tastes funny."

Mother's focus shifted to her husband. "Tell her to eat her

chowder. I didn't slave away all day for nothing, you know."

Having made his point earlier, whatever it was, Burke gazed out the French doors and said, "Maybe she's had enough."

"Nonsense! She's just picking at it. Tell her to eat her chowder."

"Mother, eat your chowder."

Eugenia offered a friendly, useless grin.

"Mother, *please*." Annoyed, Burke turned to him. "Son? Think you could lend a hand here?"

Reluctantly Parker dipped the spoon in the bowl, held it up to Eugenia's pinched lips. "It tastes funny," she said, but opened her mouth anyway. For a moment all rancor was gone, the dining room bathed in a warm nostalgic glow; he felt watchful eyes upon him as he dabbed a napkin to her wrinkly chin. Without saying so, everyone was struck by the wonder of it all: Parker was home.

4

Hours later he had another look in the bathroom mirror, but it was no more gratifying than before. Now there was a fine glaze of deceit over the weary eyes and ragged beard. He'd chosen to lie at the dinner table, even with the best of intentions, and managed only to spark a family fight. Is this what I'm coming home to? he wondered. There was the chance he'd brought it with him.

The second floor was quiet, everyone asleep, but a light was visible from Walt's room. Peering inside, he saw Walt seated cross-legged on the floor amid a mess of rags, socket wrenches, and old clothes used as rags. The walls were painted a queasy yellow, bare except for two small photographs tacked above the unmade bed.

Walt swiveled on his hips to look at him. "Yeah? What do you want?"

"Just to say goodnight." He leaned in to see what was concealed by Walt's thick neck and broad shoulders: a large rotary engine on a patch of grease-stained tarpaulin. "What's that?"

Walt blinked. "What's it look like?"

"Some kind of engine."

"Not 'some kind'! That's a Continental A-65." He pointed at it like a teacher impatient with class. "See, there's the turbine. That's the compressor. This here's the combustion chamber."

"And?"

"And *what?*"

"Where's the airplane? I heard you were building it with your bare hands."

He was having a good time needling him, until Walt rose from the floor to his full height. He'd inherited Burke's lumbering physique, standing a good half-inch taller than Parker, descended from leaner stock.

"I never said that," he said. A quick glimpse at the engine as if to assure it all is well, then he turned back with a suspicious frown. "I know why you came back."

"Is that right?"

"Wasn't 'cause you missed us. Was 'cause of the money."

Parker looked at him, befuddled. "The money . . . "

But Walt's attention veered off, coming to rest on the glossy magazine photographs tacked on the wall: in one, a Polynesian girl in a bamboo skirt frolicked on the sand, while in the other rows of giant stone heads loomed out of a windswept hillside—"carved," the caption underneath read, "in *tufa* (volcanic stone)."

When Walt looked up at him again, his eyes were dreamy and sad.

"Get out," he said.

Opening the door to his own dark room, Parker sensed right away that nothing inside had changed. Moonlight spilled through the window, trapping the walnut desk and kettle-front bureau in a harsh arctic light. Nailed to the headboards of the bed were faded newspaper clippings of childhood heroes, southpaws and astronauts. The room was a museum piece, frozen in time.

He dropped on his old bed fully clothed, tired and drunk, morally confused. No time seemed to pass between trembling in the cold room and reliving the cold sweats that came over him six months ago in LAX, that stayed with him through the ordeal of getting through customs in Tijuana, sullen inspectors unaware of money hidden under his jeans, $50,000 US strapped and sealed to his inner thigh. A long turbulent flight ended with a bone-jarring landing in Mexico City. When he finally deplaned, his leg was soaked with sweat; if money could melt there would have been a $50,000 puddle at his feet.

"One more thing," J-P had said prior to his departure. "In Mexico City you're staying with a dear friend, a lovely woman, an *artiste*, very smart, very friendly, generous to a fault. But not, er, 'up for grabs,' *comprenez-vous?*"

"Not a problem," Parker had assured him.

But Lupita was sweet on him from the start, coming to his rescue on the day he arrived, when he got into a shouting match with a cabdriver in front of her place. His tip in the cabdriver's opinion was inadequate, and he tugged at Parker's arm to emphasize his point. "*No dineros!*" Parker said, turning his pockets inside-out as evidence. "See? *Nada.*" He had plenty of *dineros,* of course, but knew enough about things not to go dipping into it for spare change. Lupita appeared from behind a sun-bleached adobe gate, flashing thousand-peso notes at the cabdriver who gratefully accepted and backed off at the same time, awed by her spiked hair, shocking red lips, overall take-no-bullshit air of Mexican aristocracy. She led Parker through a shaded courtyard and upstairs to her *piso*—high ceilings, Berber carpeting, many of her own paintings displayed on the walls. And a view from her third floor balcony that stretched from the cobblestone streets of her neighborhood, San Angel, to the distant home of wealthy *capitalistas* and beyond, almost to the outskirts of the city where untold numbers of squatter families made their homes in cardboard boxes.

The next thing he knew he was reclining in a lounge chair and sipping tequila with much of the world's largest city available for viewing. Add to this a beautiful tough-looking woman in tight jeans and paint-speckled blouse kneeling beside him, slowly removing his boot. Warm artistic fingers caressed his ankle, drifting languidly up his leg under the jeans; when her hand reached the money strap he thought he might explode. Shhhh, Lupita whispered in his ear, *hay tiempo para eso.* Time for that later.

The next few weeks he shared with her—strolling the floating gardens of Xochilmilco, helping her sell her art in Plaza San Jacinto, hitting the dance clubs of the Zona Rosa—passed like a dream. Finally the day came when he was beckoned home. They stood outside her *piso,* where it had all started, waiting for a cab. At the last minute Lupita seemed to recognize what she'd soon be missing. "My precious one," she said, touching his cheek, and left it at that. So did he. On the ride to the airport, the smoky, exhaust-throttled landscape blurred in his vision, and the cabdriver politely ignored his sobbing.

Thump! He snapped awake, listening first to silence and then another muffled *thump!* from somewhere in the house. It drew him out of the room and down the hall, where the *thumps* were softer, more rhythmic, rising from the ground floor. Quietly he followed the sounds downstairs.

In the living room, all the chairs had been set aside, the tattered Persian rug rolled up to expose smooth hardwood floor—and Rita in a petal-blue nightgown that fell to her ankles, waltzing in and out of ribbons of moonlight. As he watched, she raised her knee to the side, unfolded her leg in the air, gliding forward on the tips of her toes. Then a slow figure eight, arms lifted as if for an invisible partner, humming all the while contentedly to herself. It took his breath away.

Sensing him in mid-twirl, she stopped. "You scared me."

"Sorry."

Her face was flushed, strands of her dark hair over her forehead. She turned away, abruptly indifferent to his presence. He joined her at the bay window facing the front yard.

"It's funny," she said. "I was thinking about the lake today. That time we went out in the canoe, when we were kids."

Ghost Lake, a freshwater reservoir ten miles south of town. He hadn't thought of it in years.

"One of the paddles fell in the water and you jumped in after it, even though I begged you not to. Then you came up splashing around like you were drowning and I got scared and jumped in, too—" She laughed. "It was just a joke, big brother teasing little sister. Remember? I was mad at you for a week."

He laughed with her, unable to recall this particular incident. At the same time he grew conscious of her translucent eyes scrutinizing him. "What?"

"You look so different."

"How?"

"I don't know. It must be the beard."

She touched his chin, finding its contours under the beard. Heat seemed to radiate from her fingers, from her whole body, maybe from the exertions of dancing, but still an amazing source of heat, he thought, in this fucking cold weather.

Again she turned to look outside. The moon hung in the sky, illuminating fruit bats flitting in and out of the rock elm's upper branches.

"In some places," she said, "people leave fruits and vegetables outside at night and let the food soak up the rays of the moon. They say it helps you live a longer life."

In some places, he thought, with the memory of the painfully dysfunctional family dinner fresh in his mind, that might be a good thing. All he could say was, "Did we always used to fight this much?"

"Who?"

"You know. Like at dinner."

"Oh. I think we're really nervous, maybe because you're here." She looked at him. "Are you married, or anything like that?"

"No," he said, surprised.

"But you have a girlfriend, right? A lover?"

He thought about all that had transpired since Mexico

City—no way to put it in words she could understand. "Not anymore."

"Why did you come home?"

"I told you at dinner. I wanted to see you—all of you."

"But why now?"

So many answers to this question, none of them worth a damn. "Seemed like a good idea," he told her.

A moment passed; then she whirled away again, humming softly as she tilted and swept across the floor in ever-widening concentric circles, the thumps he'd heard earlier no more than the whisper of her feet on the hardwood floor.

Together they perceived an alien presence in the doorway: Burke with his hands in the pockets of his smoking jacket, watching.

"Time for bed, dear."

She rushed past him and upstairs. Burke followed, and a short time later, Parker, too, slipping upstairs at a safe distance. From the landing he could see them down the hall in front of her bedroom door. Perched up on her toes, Rita kissed him—short enough for an affectionate goodnight, long enough to suggest murkier possibilities. She retreated into her room. Burke stood briefly in apparent contemplation, then turned the corner, gone, too.

Parker stared into darkness, feeling white and empty, like the moon.

5

His first night home Parker dreamed of a childhood pet, the red-and-green scaled mud turtle he'd plucked from swamp marshes deep in the woods and deposited in a terrarium in his room. One night as he lay in bed reading box scores, the turtle got away. He'd released it just to let it stretch its legs, and now it was gone. He searched every room in the house and found nothing. Hours later, frantic, he stood in the living room with his head pressed to the wall, a very faint clawing sound inside the wall causing his ear to sizzle like a live wire; it was the sound of his turtle. Somehow it had crawled into the attic and tumbled down between girders, lodged now among jutting chunks of plaster. To Parker, aged eight, the solution was clear: call a wrecking crew and tear out the wall. His pleas were sadly refused. Huddled in the dark, in his pajamas, he listened to his wounded companion call out to him in a tiny frightened turtle voice.

Soon after, the feeble scratching stopped. Mother took him

upstairs and put him to bed, explaining with a shrug that there was nothing anyone could do.

Years later, encountering losses of a greater magnitude, he remembered the mud turtle and his mother's helpless shrug. *Nothing anyone could do.*

Waking to bright shafts of sunlight, he stumbled to the bathroom, showered, then had one last look at himself in the mirror. The face looking back at him was haunted and wild, like a mad Russian monk. Maybe it *was* the beard.

Once conceded, the rest came easy. With a razor from the medicine cabinet and Walt's scented shave cream, the process took little time. Soon the clean jaw of a new man looked back at him. His eyes shed their cast-iron sheen—years in fact had vanished with each stroke of the blade. Here was a kind face, a face you could trust.

In his room, dressing by the window, he watched a flock of Canada geese carve a triangle in the northern sky. An omen, he decided, of better things to come.

"'Bout time you got up."

It was Walt in flannel shirt and overalls taking up the doorway. A long time passed with no reaction. Then Walt said, "I was wondering what your plans might be."

"You mean, for the rest of my life?"

"I'm talking about today."

Rita met them in the hall wearing a thick wool sweater pulled down over jeans. Parker modeled his new look for her.

"What do you think? Walt didn't even notice."

"Notice what?" Walt said.

Rita stared at him intently; unnerved by her wide-eyed silence he turned on Walt, pointing at his own face. "This," he said. "Me."

"I—I noticed." Walt blinked behind his glasses. "Just didn't feel like saying nothing."

She continued to stare, as if examining him for scientific purposes.

"Well?"

"I was just getting used to the beard," she said.

Walt led them downstairs into the hall and out the front door. When he stepped outside, a shock of cold air slapped him across his clean-shaven face. He stayed on the front porch with Rita, while Walt pushed through snowdrifts to start up his truck.

"Where are we going?"

"To dance class. I try to go early so I can get home and keep an eye on things."

He shivered in his lightweight jacket. "It's cold."

"You're just not used to it," she said. "Look at the frost on the trees, how clear and sharp everything is. Didn't you once all that time you were away miss winter back at home?"

The evergreens surrounding the house did have a hard beauty, even as he felt his lips turning blue. But he couldn't remember a time—not lying poolside in Topanga Canyon or passing through Mexican customs with a small fortune strapped to his leg, or even when he was on his knees in the dirt getting the shit beat out of him south of the border—not one time could he recall being drawn to, or stirred by, memories of home.

"Sure I did," he said.

In the driveway Walt's truck sputtered unwillingly to life. Rita hopped through fluffy snow and climbed in, but Parker didn't follow. Along the side of the house he saw Burke hard at work at something by the low stone wall; at the same moment the old man turned and saw him, and now he beckoned him over.

Funny, he thought, how your first instinct is to run. In the truck Walt was preoccupied with keeping the engine alive, Rita gazing out at empty fields. So he negotiated a path through snow that came at him in waves, knee-high and higher, while overhead the dull gray sky brooded like a problem child.

Burke knelt on a patch of hard ground, hammering a length of arrowhead barbed wire onto the old stone wall. As he crossed the yard, Parker saw for the first time that coiled barbed-wire covered the wall in three directions, even entangled in the swinging gate in the driveway. The sight of it caught him up short and for a moment he had to brace himself against the rock elm's flinty bark, as a rush of unpleasant sensations washed over him—the warm lips of the twelve-gauge kissing his chest, the awful buried memory of a turtle lodged deep inside a wall. When his head finally cleared, he trudged the remaining distance and came up beside Burke—or, actually, over him kneeling by the wall.

"Everything OK? You looked a bit woozy there."

"I'm fine," Parker said.

His stepfather's black bombardier jacket and snug-fitting watch cap had a certain jaunty quality, all out of place here in the frozen tundra. "Where's everyone headed?"

"Town."

"You too?"

He nodded. "I don't get it," he said. "Are you trying to keep someone out or locking someone in?"

"Can't have our defenses penetrated as easily as you did yesterday." Burke stared up at him. "I see you've taken the blade to yourself."

"What? Oh, yeah—for Mother."

Burke stood, brushing snow off his pants. A gust of wind swept over the yard. "While you're here, what do you say to a little hunting?"

"No thanks," Parker said. "I don't hunt."

"Oh? Is this due to some lofty moral standard or maybe you just can't shoot worth a damn?"

It was too early in the day and too damn cold for this. A truck horn pierced the air: Walt, glaring at them through the windshield.

"About your brother," Burke said. "You may have noticed the chip on his shoulder. How he always seems to be spoiling for a fight."

"I thought it was just me."

"No, he's fairly indiscriminate." Burke spoke in an oddly confidential tone, though they were far out of hearing range. "My belief is he suffers from some sort of brain damage, possibly incurred at birth. Something's a shade off in here—" A finger pointing at his forehead rotated in lazy circles. "A shade . . . *twisted*. I expect you as the oldest sibling to make allowances."

The free-floating dread inspired by the sight of barbed wire fused into a single observation: the old man was nuts. Spooked,

Parker took a step backward in the snow.

"Son, have I told you yet how happy we are to have you back home with us?"

"No," he said, still moving away. "You haven't."

For a while in the truck no one spoke. Walt stared ahead behind the wheel, Rita quiet beside him, Parker looking out at rolling fields covered in white and frozen saplings bent close to the road. Rockbridge was ten miles away, a factory town of gas stations, banks, hardware stores. Children from outlying farms attended school there, along with the sons and daughters of machinists; growing up, he had few friends among them, and lacked any excitement about seeing them again. As the pickup sped past clapboard farmhouses, an occasional Pontiac up on blocks, it felt like they were driving back through time.

"Something's bothering you," Rita said. "A dream . . . is that it?"

He looked sideways at her.

"No, don't tell me." Closing her eyes, she instructed him to do the same. "OK. Give me an image."

"Give you—?"

"Just do it," Walt said.

So he closed his eyes, settled into the bumpy rhythms of the truck and just for the hell of it imagined his turtle's headlong dive into darkness, the crush of timber beams and slow solitary death.

"Are you thinking?"

"Yeah."

"Something's falling," she said, "something green, with little feet and a little head and a, a—"

"Shell," Parker said, and bit his lip.

She tugged at Walt's elbow. "The turtle! Remember the turtle Parker used to keep in his room?"

"Y'mean, the one that fell inside the wall?" Walt laughed without sympathy. "Nothing like coming home to stir up all them memories, huh?"

Smiling bravely, he tried to joke it away. "Can you predict the future too?"

Rita blushed. Walt snarled at him. "She's got a gift, OK? Nobody around here knows and we want to keep it that way."

"Walt says it's like the inner spirits that gave the natives strength to build those giant stone heads."

"Which natives?" Parker asked. "What heads?"

"The ones on Easter Island."

"*Rapa Nui,*" Walt said, tightening his grip on the wheel. "I wish you'd get that right."

She waved a hand over the winter landscape, as if dismissing it. "Did you know they have wild horses there? I can't wait to see them."

"Why are we talking about Easter Island?"

"We're not," Walt snapped. "Forget it."

The truck began a long descent out of woodland and onto two-lane blacktop, recently plowed and less jarring of a ride. At the first hint of physical comfort, Parker suffered a belated attack of conscience regarding his theatrics over dinner the night before. He squirmed in his seat.

"You know that stuff I said at the table last night? I may have been stretching the truth a little here and there."

"You could have told us anything," Rita said, "and we'd believe you. We don't know what's going on out there, do we, Walt?"

"Nope. Don't want to, either." He glanced at Parker, annoyed. "Hey, whiz kid, wanna know what life's like for *us*? Could we maybe interest you in that topic for a minute or two?"

"Sure."

"Old man's off hunting mostly, we don't see him sometimes for days. Mother goes into town, shopping and whatnot. Rita takes her classes and me—when I need money, I fix engines. Ain't flashy, I admit, but we get by."

Rita added, with a brazen smile: "Not flashy's OK, too."

"Absolutely," Walt agreed.

The pickup crossed a narrow bridge spanning a riverbed encased in ice. Fresh tracks, fox or muskrat, appeared in the dusting of surface snow below.

"Fuck it," Walt said, and stepped on the gas. They drove past rusty tool-sheds, a cemetery, three crumbling barns in a hurry.

"You're driving too fast," Rita said.

"Back at the house," Walt said, ignoring her, "the old man was talking about me, right? Told you something happened when I was a kid—"

Parker felt her growing tense beside him.

"Told you I had brain damage, didn't he?"

"Slow down," Parker said.

"Didn't he?" Outside, a blur of telephone poles. "He thinks I'm retarded! They both do!" His hands flew off the steering wheel. "You too!"

Up ahead the road veered sharply out of sight—barely time

enough to feel a stab of terror over what might be coming the other way. Brakes, windshield, pain, blood. But somehow the truck took the curve and now they careened down a flat stretch of pavement, roaring past a sign ROCKBRIDGE CITY LIMITS and snowy pastures with cattle standing around uselessly in the snow.

"Retarded!"

Directly in front of them, a black-and-white-spotted heifer stumbled through a broken fence into the middle of the road, watching the truck barrel down with perfect bovine serenity.

Parker reached over and, seizing the wheel, tugged violently left. The truck went into a spin, missing the placid cow by inches, while in motion presenting a giddy merry-go-round view of fence posts, utility poles, boundless miles of snow. Tires crashed into underbrush, swiveling toward a muddy drainage ditch. For a moment the hood buckled up and all he could see was empty sky; then the pickup slammed to earth at the edge of the ditch, engine wheezing from the effort before collapsing completely.

Time passed. Sounds of life in the country—a hound's yelp, the clash and scatter of crows—gradually resumed. Walt sat behind the wheel breathing hard, Rita apparently unharmed but looking close to tears. Parker stared out the windshield, dizzy with adrenaline.

"Not retarded," he finally announced. "*Twisted,* is what he said."

"Twisted?" Walt yanked off the glasses and rubbed his eyes hard, like a man in a sandstorm. "Who? Me?"

6

The Red Hawk Diner was brightly lit and empty at this early hour, except for a sleepy-eyed factory worker at the counter and a middle-aged waitress flirting with the cook through a panel in the wall separating kitchen from diner. A feed-lot calendar on the wall—September, 1981—was two months out of date. Parker sat facing Walt in a booth of cracked leather. Above them, speckled trout were mounted alongside oil paintings of Pope John Paul and U.S. Representative Thomas P. "Tip" O'Neil, Jr.

"Scared the hell outa you, didn't he?"

"What?"

"I saw what happened to the window," Walt said. "When the old man's packing I always steer clear."

Parker looked out the window at Main Street, the sky fouled by thick layers of fumes from the paper mill north of town. Of course the moment was still with him, the radiant light and deafening roar, the awful certainty he'd been gut-shot, a bullet fragmenting his vital organs. And after realizing he was unharmed, the worst memory of all—dropping to the floor, mashing his face against a chair, Ajax snarling at him through the legs of the pool table. Humiliating.

"He didn't scare me. I knew he was kidding all along."

Walt snickered. "I bet you did."

Earlier they'd dropped Rita off at the high school gym; she ran inside with a word, where jazz-rock echoed from loudspeakers and young women in leotards unfolded their limbs on the waxy basketball court. They drove into town in silence.

It occurred to him now that his return home might not have been a surprise after all. Maybe within her veil of senility Eugenia recognized him from the start; the shotgun blast could have been a test, or warning of some kind. *Stranger, stay away.* All he knew for sure was that things had got off on the wrong foot and he shared some of the blame for that. He hoped there was time to set things right.

"Hell of a mess if I hit that cow," Walt said.

"Yeah, but we would've had hamburger for a month."

They shared a rare laugh as the waitress delivered Walt's breakfast: hotcakes, Denver omelet, hash browns, side order of whole wheat toast, lightly buttered. The name-tag on her uniform pocket read MOLLY. She asked Parker, "Sure you don't want something, honey?"

His appetite after the joy-ride to town was gone. "Coffee's fine."

Molly's rubber-soled shoes squeaked away on the checkerboard linoleum floor.

"Talk about brain damage." Walt sprayed bits of bacon and

green pepper as he spoke. "Don't come any more damaged than *his*."

"Looks like he's not getting along too well with Mother."

"You could say that," Walt said. "You *could* say they hate each other's guts, and Mother hates Eugenia and we all know for a fact the old man hates *me*—" Seeing Parker's distressed look, he laughed. "See? I'm just kidding, too!"

You may have noticed the chip on his shoulder. That was Walt all right—sullen one minute, goofy and hyperactive the next. I can handle him, he thought. I always could.

"All I'm saying, the old man ain't any better than before—worse I think in some ways. Never gets weak and frail, y'know? Just the same old hard-ass son of a bitch making us feel all the time like we're . . . I don't know, under house arrest or something."

"You're not."

"Huh?"

Parker leaned across the table with creamy swirls inlaid in Formica. "You're not under house arrest. If it's so bad, leave. Get out like I did."

Walt squinted and held his breath, as if barely able to contain poisonous vapors within. "Lemme tell you something," he finally said. "All those years you were gone? We hardly talked about you once. Mother figured you were dead and gone, since you never wrote or called or nothing. Eugenia forgot you ever existed ten minutes after you walked out of the house."

Good, he thought, let it out. "What about you, Walt? Did you miss me?"

"I had other stuff on my mind, y'know? Like how're me

and Rita supposed to grow up all alone in the house, left to our own defenses? 'Cause you were too damn busy with your own self to care."

Letting it out was one thing, but this bitter reproach stung him. "I cared. Of course I cared. Things weren't as simple as that."

"Looks pretty simple to me. You left first chance you got."

"I left because it was time to leave."

"Oh, yeah, OK—"

"No reason you can't do the same."

Walt's fist squeezed around a fork. "What's the use of talking to you?"

"You boys want more coffee?" Molly asked from the counter. Turning in unison they said: "*No.*" She wrinkled her nose, then resumed flirting with the short-order cook.

In the booth tempers flared and receded, like fireworks. Walt finished his breakfast and pushed the plate away.

"If you fix cars," Parker said, "why is there an airplane engine in your bedroom?"

"I'm rebuilding it."

"For a plane waiting somewhere."

"I never said that." Walt glanced around the diner, focused momentarily on the factory worker who lay slumped over sleeping on the counter. "But if there *was* one, know what it'd be?"

"Nope."

"Wendt *Traveler.* Single A-65 engine, up-rated to sixty horses. She climbs to sixteen thousand feet without blinking an eye. Not a whole lot of fixed-wing tandems can do that without coming apart at the seams."

Parker was impressed. "Do you know how to fly?"

"Well, uh . . . no."

"I think that's kind of required."

"Learning to fly costs money," Walt said. "So do your spare parts and et cetera. Take for example your raw materials." Enumerating on short stubby fingers, a new mood—pride or excitement—coming over him. "There's sheet metal, steel tubing, a whole shitload of nuts and bolts. And don't forget army-navy bits and cement-coated nails with elastic stop nuts."

Parker agreed that was quite a list.

"How 'bout work space? For something that size you need room to lay the wing panels out flat—and they go thirty feet across! Where'n hell am I gonna find that kinda space?" His face darkened. "*He* could buy spare parts, if he wanted to. *He's* got the money."

"Who?"

"All I got's a busted pickup with a leak in the fuel line and carburetor shot to hell. *He* could buy spare parts. *He's* got the money."

"*Who?*"

Walt sighed, as if trying to explain logarithms to a five-year-old. "You know what I'm talking about."

He sipped coffee, his silence implying an air of old news. It seemed to work; within minutes Walt burst forth with his story. "Happened by accident," he said. "I was up in the study looking for my birth certificate, in case I wanted to go to flight school or something. But I found other stuff instead. Papers and documents about the people he used to work for, how they paid him off to keep quiet about things."

Heat rose off the nearby grill. The diner felt stuffy and enclosed. Documents?

"Burke was a civil servant buried somewhere in the State Department. What did he have to keep quiet about?"

"I *told* you. I saw the documents. Old man's got a bundle." Glancing at the counter to make sure no one was listening. "Back when he quit his spying job, he goes to the boss, tells him, I'm gonna write this exposé-type book, y'know, Who I Am and What I Did. His boss doesn't like it, it's nothing he wants the whole world to hear. So they work out a deal. The old man promises not to write the book, in exchange for which they send him something extra for his golden years."

The cook emerged from the kitchen—a squat whiskery man in a grease-stained apron—and proceeded to lay out pots and pans and other gleaming instruments on the counter. The factory worker slept on.

"That ain't even the best part!" Walt said. "Old man wrote the damn book anyway, nasty stuff, too, bribes, 'ssasinations, overthrowing foreign governments. Know what it's called?"

"No clue."

"*Our Flag Was Still There.*" He sat back beaming, as though he'd come up with the title himself. "What d'ya think of that?"

A shriek of joy drew their attention to the counter, where the cook stood juggling a meat cleaver, spatula, steel fork and long serrated knife in the air. Molly laughing and applauding.

He didn't think Walt would know a government document if the wind wrapped one around his face. Still, it made sense in a way. Throughout Parker's childhood Burke was gone much of the time, postings in Cairo, Berlin, Panama City, his job to update embassy officials on ever-changing policies and protocols. So whenever he reminisced about the good old days of guerrilla warfare and the fine art of killing a man, Parker assumed it was all made up, local color piled on a bleak, humdrum life in the diplomatic trenches. Years later, here in the Red Hawk Diner, Walt's tortured attempt at a sly grin suggested other possibilities. "I guess that means you know where it is."

"What? The book?"

"The *bundle*."

"'Course I do. In a secret bank account."

Enough, he thought. "Where's that, Walt? In the Rockbridge Savings & Loan?"

There was a crash behind them as stainless-steel implements toppled out of the juggler's orbit and landed on the floor. This woke the factory worker. "What? Who? Where's the fire?" Molly and the cook vanished from sight, the sounds they were making behind the counter turning into rude grunts and groans, animal sounds, undisguised lust. The factory worker leaned over the counter for a better look; what he saw brought a smile to his weary face.

"Don't worry," Walt said. "I know."

Given a choice he would have preferred whatever warmth he could find inside the pickup, rather than a leisurely stroll down Main Street led by Walt in his black hooded coat, indifferent to the winds chasing after them. Walt conveyed disjointed narratives concerning each shop they passed, their various contents and origins, including Nate's Five & Dime, the forlorn Sunoco station, a Greek family-owned laundry with a FOR SALE sign in the window. As if I fucking care, Parker thought.

Finally the weather was too much even for Walt; they paused beneath an awning for Dooley's Grocery.

Parker asked, "So where would you go—I mean, if you had one of those . . . What're they called again?"

"*Wendt* Traveler." Walt stood facing the street in hooded profile. "I know where I'd go. I don't see it being any of your business."

"Why not take a plane like normal people do?"

"That ain't flying," the hood said. "That's sitting cramped up next to some fat lady or guy selling life insurance. We got just this one flight to make and I wanna do it right."

"*We?*"

The hood jerked back and around, beady black eyes visible behind thick glasses. "I never said that."

"Yeah you did. You said it just now."

"Never said *we*."

He recalled glossy photos tacked to the bedroom wall—native girls dancing on sand, rows of giant stone heads—and had to laugh.

"What's so goddamn funny?"

"She's not going anywhere, sure as hell not with you."

"She'll leave," Walt told him, "if there's no more reason to stay."

The storm struck, ear-shattering blasts of sleet and wind that knocked him on his heels, sucked air from his lungs. Under the awning he watched a force of nature blow through town, Old Testament in its passion and fury, blanketing parked cars and storefronts. Telephone poles buckled, threatened to fall. Out of the maelstrom appeared a black late-model Jeep Cherokee, caught in a spin across icy asphalt and careening off a snow-covered fire hydrant—but never once, judging by the glance he caught of the driver's wild grin—any cause for concern. A final ninety-degree spin and the Jeep came to rest diagonally across three parking spaces in front of the Bijou, Rockbridge's last surviving movie theater, currently closed for repairs.

When the driver emerged a moment later, the hood came off and Walt's face lit up—a startling transformation from Neanderthal scowl to schoolboy's look of glee.

"Hey! Doctor Trunk!"

And headed into the snowstorm on Main Street before realizing Parker wasn't with him. He rushed back, yanked him free of shelter. "*Come on.*" Like plunging into an avalanche, he thought, snow pummeling his face and mid-section. The blind led the blind through the Arctic blast, but somehow the intermittently distinct figure ahead of him reached the curb and pulled him in, too, for the relative safety beneath the Bijou's weather-beaten marquee. It read TH XO CIST.

The driver smiled, a thin, middle-aged man in jeans and a sleeveless trail vest. "Hello, Walt."

"Morning, Doctor Trunk!" To Parker he announced: "This is Doctor Trunk. I do all the work on his car." And to the older man, with far less enthusiasm: "This is my uh brother. He's been away for awhile."

Trunk shook hands vigorously. "Can it be? The prodigal son here in the flesh?" He had piercing blue eyes and ash-blonde hair, a drooping mustache several shades darker. "We've heard so much about you."

The storm, having finally exhausted itself, left Rockbridge no more than an icebound Siberian outpost. Ice froze everything in place, from commercial establishments to formerly operating vehicles. The only sound came from rivulets of sludge jamming the gutters.

Trunk rummaged among the pockets of his trail vest, producing a hand-carved Meerschaum pipe and a pouch of cherry tobacco. "So you've come in out of the cold, as it were. In search of those warm home fires."

His tone held the mocking echo of distant college days; Parker, still grappling with freshly divulged family secrets, didn't care for it. "Yeah, something like that."

"Tell you what. Let me call the mayor—he's a close personal friend—set up a homecoming parade down Main Street. Cheerleaders, marching band, the whole nine yards." He lit the pipe with a long-stemmed kitchen match. "How's that sound?"

"Like too much trouble on my account."

"Don't be so goddamn sensitive," Walt snapped. "Doctor Trunk's just being friendly."

Parker met the older man's steady gaze. This family stuff, it's put him off. "OK."

Trunk turned to Walt and for several minutes they talked in an odd hushed intimacy, dropping terms like "downwash" and "parasitic drag." He began to feel purposely excluded.

"What kind of doctor?" he interrupted.

Trunk's smile exposed teeth of uncanny whiteness beneath the walrus mustache. "Pee-aitch-dee," he said, enunciating each syllable. "I teach."

"What? What do you teach?"

"Paleoanthropology."

"Out here?" he said, inexplicably nettled. "In the middle of nowhere?"

Trunk looked up and down Main Street, as if embarrassed by his reply. "Harvard, actually."

"So this is like being out in the field, right? Observing Early Franklin County Man in his native habitat?"

"I happen to be on sabbatical at the moment. Not doing much of anything."

Walt sneered. "My brother can be a real asshole sometimes."

"Fuck this." Parker turned, fully prepared to walk ten miles home in the snow. A reassuring hand fell on his shoulder.

"Hot-tempered, are we? Please—stay."

He stayed.

"An apology's in order," Trunk said. "You see, in the university, survival depends on having an air of absolute authority, if only to intimidate your students and keep your esteemed yet bloodthirsty colleagues at bay." He paused to relight the pipe. "By the time tenure rolls around, this air of authority has become a permanent part of your make-up like, say, brittle fingernails or curvature of the spine. If at times I appear cryptic or superficially hostile, well, it's only with people I like. I guess when you get right down to it, I'm just too damn shy."

Parker looked at the stoplight over the intersection, a red-and-green flashing block of ice. It didn't sound like much of an apology to him.

"Just ignore him," Walt said. "He's the moody type."

Trunk waved it away. "I'm having a little get-together at my place tomorrow night—nothing fancy, just a few friends from out of town. Would you boys like to come?"

"A party? At your house?" Walt was breathless. "Really?"

"And bring that young sister of yours . . . What's her name again?"

"Rita. Yeah, sure. Whatever you say."

"Fine. See you then." Trunk tapped the bowl of the pipe against an upturned heel, replaced smoking accessories in various vest pockets, then ambled off down Main Street, oblivious to anxious shopkeepers emerging for a peek at storm damage. Parker watched him go, a man at peace with the icebound world. What the hell was *that* about?

Suddenly Walt's blunt, seething face pressed close to his.

"Don't ever pull a stunt like that again, hear me? That man is a fucking *genius*."

7

"Forgot somethin' at the hardware store," Walt said, behind the wheel. "See you at the gym."

Parker walked down three blocks of Main Street, past the Rockbridge P.O. and Sunoco station and age-old barber shop with a wavy red-and-white-striped pole in front—left-over, Eugenia once told him, from the days when bloodletting was performed there. He scanned passersby in heavy winter garb, hoping to spot a familiar face. There weren't any.

The Bay State Bar & Grill was the last business in town. He ducked inside, ordered a beer from the stony-faced bartender. Scattered customers—all male, all wearing grain caps or Red Sox caps, all questionable-looking in one way or another—sat at rickety tables. A clock over the bar flashed "Pilsner" in neon along with the time: not quite noon. He thought: One little drink never hurt anybody.

At first, however, beer offered little solace from his brooding thoughts and the Bay State's crepuscular ambience. It bothered him not knowing how much truth there was, if any, in Walt's revelations. Government documents, secret bank accounts, a mysterious tell-all manuscript. All this while the clearly disturbed man in question was busy, ten miles away, hammering a barbed-wire barricade around the house. *And Mother hates Eugenia, and we all know for a fact the old man hates me.* He sighed in his beer. Just a couple of days home and already it felt like slogging through mud.

"This winter ain't so bad," a stocky man said at the end of the bar. "Not compared to the great storm of '75."

The bartender nodded somberly, wiping glasses.

"Forty below, snow up to your chin. Hell of a frigging storm. They had schooners locked in drift ice five miles offshore and nobody could get at them. Men starved to death in plain sight of land."

Parker couldn't recall this devastating winter. "Schooners? In '75?"

With a nod at the bartender, who finally cracked a smile, the man said, "1875."

Over the next beer he imagined Rita seated beside him, smiling and beautiful in a white summer dress. At a nearby table the crew of an abandoned schooner, rescued miraculously after weeks at sea, eyes her hungrily. Lust turns palpable; one by one the deranged seamen rise from the table and advance on them. Parker cracks a bottle on the edge of the bar, radiating genuine menace. The crew backs away. He exits with Rita on his arm, and all is well.

"Thanks," he said to the bartender on the way out. "I needed that."

After a handful of tree-lined streets, Rockbridge faded into an unincorporated region of corrugated shacks and trailer parks. The unpaved road he walked on dropped into a small ravine; a rusted drain-pipe fed into a creek, everything in the creek—weeds, rocks, bits and pieces of scrap metal—trapped in ice.

He took a cautious step forward, expecting spidery cracks to erupt under his boot. But the ice held and he made it across by skidding, without much grace. Looking back, he saw the curled neck of a black plumber's snake sticking out of the ice and suddenly he was thrust back into the clamor and noise of the Tijuana airport six months ago, standing exhausted and bleary-eyed after a long connecting flight from Mexico City. Something poked his spine; he turned to face a short man in a loud Hawaiian shirt, tugging at his sleeve and entreating him—*Por favor* and *ven el carro, senor* over and over—in a not altogether friendly way. On his neck, a tattooed rattlesnake with scales, fangs and forked tongue. Parker backed away explaining, *No, gracias,* he wasn't getting in anybody's car, when another man's forearm shot across his throat from behind and he fell back clawing at the arm that slowly, insistently pressed off his air supply. In this way he ended up outside the terminal and in the back of a waiting car, things happening too fast for any eyewitnesses to notice or care.

As the car roared off, his wrists were tied, a hood draped over his head. Foolishly he attempted to negotiate—*A mistake, senor,* some kind of—and a fist as thick and dense as cinder-block struck the side of his head. Parker was quiet after that.

City noises faded. By the drop in temperature and rich

smell of sagebrush, he guessed they were speeding through the desert at night. Angry voices quarreled in front, too fast to understand except in snatches. *Y ahora que vamos a hacer? Matarlo?* What are we supposed to do? Kill him? Who? he thought. Kill who? The driver said, *dejalo aqui de abajo del sol* and the other agreed, *el sol lo acaba*. The sun will finish him off. He gave way to panic, hurling his trussed-up body against the back of the passenger seat and thrusting its unseen occupant hard against the dashboard. Tires screeched, car doors flew open. Brutal hands wrenched him out and tossed him in the dirt. The hood came off; he squinted into headlights, saw nothing.

At first the men stood there haranguing him, shouting abuse in his bewildered face—*Pendejo! Cabrón! Hijo de puta!*—and then the beating began in earnest. Fists rained down on his head, steel-tipped boots kicked at kidneys and spleen, in spite of his best efforts to roll into a ball to protect himself. There was blood and dust in his mouth, parts of his body floating off in a surfeit of pain. Now he was raised to his knees, looking through swollen eyes at the man with the rattlesnake tattoo, speaking calmly to him, repeating a name that made no sense in this particular time and place. At some point, mercifully, he passed out.

Climbing out of the little ravine was harder than it looked; when he finally traversed the hard slick ground, he came upon the old athletic field and beyond, Calvin Coolidge High, a squat ugly fifties-era structure with darkened windows and a caked tar roof. In the distance, two boys attempted to scale the icy goal-posts. Otherwise, the place seemed terribly deserted.

Get out, he told himself. Pack up and get out . . . again.

A short time later he stood outside the doors of the high school gym as young women in leotards went through cooling-down exercises as loudspeakers garbled a Bach concerto. Rita, clearly the prettiest girl there, twirled to the faulty lilt of violins, oblivious to everything but the practiced flow of her arms and legs.

"Nice girl," a gruff voice said behind him.

It was Alf Cooper, stocky and jovial in uniform and badge. "That your little sister in there? She sure has grown."

After seeing Alf the last time, he'd nearly got gutshot for breaking and entering. It seemed like something to mention, but then he thought better of it.

"Used to come to town in the old days, buy up all my sweet corn. That's the first time I noticed her."

"Rita?"

"Your mother," Alf said. "Always saved my best ears for her."

Inside the gym, exercises were over; some girls toweled off by the bleachers while others, Rita included, headed for the lockers. Outside, Alf's friendly manner gave way to a grim aspect.

"Things go bad sometimes," he said, "I can't deny it. First it looks like a cakewalk down the aisle, nothing but blue skies and roses ahead. Next thing you know it's twenty years on and there ain't no more reason to smile. Feels more like incarceration, y'know? A goddamn matrimonial house of corrections!" Veins bulged in his neck, flesh reddening around the shirt collar. "You!" he cried, pointing at Parker. "You're the smart one, you tell me! What good ever came of a situation like that?"

He couldn't begin to decipher this tirade, but "No good" seemed like a safe answer. A fat raindrop fell on his head. Clouds were massing in the sky, another storm on the way. He opened the door and stepped inside the gym, but Alf chose not to follow.

"Parker!"

He turned to see Rita on the basketball court, a wool sweater tied over her shoulders, cardigan skirt wrapped over her leotards. When he looked outside again, Alf Cooper was gone.

She spun Parker around, gave him an exuberant kiss. "Right on time!"

"No—I mean, Walt's not here yet, he—"

Shrill honking came from the pickup not ten feet away in the parking lot.

"You're teasing! There he is right now."

Walt was yelling, his words if not his chronically agitated tone of voice muffled by the windshield and fast-breaking storm.

"—hell are you are you waiting for! Can't you see it's raining?"

A steady downpour followed them home, cold rain falling slantwise through the trees. The truck hit gaping potholes at high speed and he feared another hair-raising ride; but Rita beside him cheerfully recounted events from dance class, including Mrs. Spoto, the instructor, praising her *pas de deux*, "though of course that was with another girl 'cause there's no boys in the class."

Cold, wet, hungry, Parker didn't hear. He blamed Walt for his festering bad mood, while Walt for his part kept his eyes on the road; soon they arrived at the house. Walt left the idling pickup to slosh through snow and swing open the barbed-wire gate, which didn't even draw a comment from anyone.

Rita stared dead ahead, but spoke softly to him. "You're glad to be home," she said.

"What?"

"You don't know it, but you are." Her face remained in profile. "I just wanted you to know."

" . . . Thanks."

Walt climbed in and eased the truck ahead over gravel and snow, stopping by the side of the house. He cut the engine, looked over at Parker.

"That stuff I told you back in the Red Hawk . . ."

"What about it?"

"Forget it. It ain't really none of your business. You're just passing through."

"But what if you're telling the truth?" Parker asked him. "There's always that possibility."

Walt's grin could be seen as insolent, simple-minded or just plain mean. "I guess that's how it goes talking to someone with *brain damage*. You can't ever tell for sure."

Enough, he thought. Anything was better than listening to this crap. He opened the side door and stepped into the rain. Strange sounds drifted to his ears, a series of low moans floating in and out of the wind, slowly blossoming to a glass-shattering scream.

He leaned down to the window. "Did you hear that?"

Rita and Walt looked blank.

Another scream cut through the air; there was no time to think about it. Rushing up the sidewalk, he hurtled the porch steps and opened the front door. At first the house was quiet with that deep, embedded silence of early afternoons; then a scream rose from the kitchen, animal-like in its impenetrable woe. He ran down the hall without thinking to prepare himself for what he might see. The actual carnage—chairs up-ended, dishes cracked, saucepot spilling over on the stove, gobs of fettuccini sliding down summer-blue wallpaper—was fairly overwhelming. And Mother sprawled across the breakfast table, her flowery apron splashed with blood, arms and legs flailing like a victim of hit-and-run.

Eugenia stood over her, a steel soup ladle in her upraised hand. "Ha!" she cried. "Didn't see *that* one coming, did you?"

2

THICKER THAN WATER

8

The morning after the beating, he woke to grinding pain in every extremity, so pervasive and severe that for a long time he could do no more than blink. Clothes torn, shoeless, alone in a sweeping vista of tumbleweed and scarecrow-shaped cacti. Vultures circled overhead. Blinding sun roasted his body. *El sol lo acaba.*

At some point a car appeared on the low-slung horizon, rolling out of a dust storm as a Lincoln Continental, black, with dark-tinted windows, slowing to a stop a short distance away—as if the passengers inside were debating whether or not to get out and help him. What are you waiting for? he thought. Because I can't fucking walk to you.

At last a blonde woman in a nurse's starched white uniform emerged from the Lincoln, crossing the torrid desert floor in crepe-soled shoes. She knelt close and spoke to him in the reassuring cadence of his native tongue. He was unable to reply. Instead he let her lift him to his feet like a helpless drunk and guide him to the waiting luxury vehicle; tumbling backward onto plush leather, he fell in love with the nurse's dyed roots and experienced anew the miracle of air-conditioning. The bull-necked driver never turned around to look.

His recovery took place in a small, modestly furnished room with fringed lamps and a gossamer-curtained window. It was locked, as was the door. Over time he came to understand that the subject wasn't open for discussion. The Guatemalan housekeeper, a squat dark-skinned woman with scowling eyebrows, vacuumed, cleaned the toilet, never spoke. Once a week he was a visited by a jaunty man in a tweed jacket calling himself Doctor Jones ("Tell Doctor where it hurts" and "Doctor Jones is first and foremost concerned with your health"), who kept him hopped up on sedatives and massive infusions of vitamin B. Acceptable topics for discussion included small talk about the weather, the state of his recuperation, and a prized collection of South American tree frogs the doctor sometimes brought along on his rounds, rows of tiny green frogs pinned, stretched and mounted in a gilt-frame case.

Gradually the medical visits lessened, as did the dulling effects of pain-killers. He listened more closely to sounds outside the window, water trickling into an unseen pool, voices young and old accompanied by flapping beach-clogs and squeaky inflatable toys. Over droning traffic, the syrupy whisper of waves. He grew stronger. Pain receded to tolerable levels. Soon he could hobble to the bathroom on his own—checking the door each time, always locked—wondering yet again who was behind his enforced convalescence and what was expected of him. His true task, he decided, was to stay alert, wait for the day Doctor Jones or the phlegmatic mestizo housekeeper forgot and left the door unlocked. One day, one of them did.

A narrow balcony opened to a cobblestone breakfast nook one floor down, with wrought-iron tables and a gently splashing fountain nestled in bougainvillea. There was no one around. Throwing a robe over his boxer shorts, Parker headed away from what he guessed was the lobby, passing instead through a short tunnel between buildings that gave way to a rooftop patio resplendent with sunlight. Gulls flocked noisily overhead. He smelled cotton candy and sun-tan lotion. Beyond a row of beachfront summer rentals, he had a far-reaching view of the Pacific ocean.

A long-haired kid rolled by on a skateboard in the alley below. "Hey!" Parker yelled. "Where am I?" And got a middle-finger salute for an answer.

A deck chair and recliner had been baking in the sun all day. He dropped onto hot vinyl, oblivious to the shock to his sun-starved body, and closed his eyes. Ambient beach noise carried him off to a *colonia* in Mexico City, strolling through the farmer's market with Lupita, making love with her under the lazy revolutions of a batik ceiling fan . . .

"Bonjour, mon ami."

His eyes closed, he could still believe this was part of the dream; certainly the ponderous scent of Mediterranean after-shave and Old World tobacco was vivid enough for it. But when he looked over, there was no mistaking the lanky figure beside him, the grooved scar on the cheekbone and supernatural shade of black hair. Stretched out on the deck chair as if they'd been hanging out all day, kicking over old times.

"I caught you dreaming, *oui?* About a woman, I bet."

"I don't think so." He sat up, rubbing his face. "It had something to do with going home."

Jean-Paul said, "I don't believe you've ever said where home is."

The sun wouldn't release him from drowsiness, at a moment when he dimly understood it was critical to keep his wits about him. "Back east."

"*Où là?* Exactly?"

"Wheeling," he said, hoping it didn't sound as random as it was. "Wheeling, West Virginia."

J-P shook a cigarette from a pack of Gaulois and lit it. "Whee-ling," he repeated in a sing-song voice. "And Lupita? How are things with her?"

"Things with her . . ." After inventing humble origins in Appalachia, he was fresh out of ideas. "Things are fine."

Which turned out to be the right answer, since J-P leaned back and smoked contemplatively, leaving him to stew in his own paranoid juices. The unannounced appearance, while going a long way toward explaining the situation, didn't augur well.

Despite the silk monogrammed shirt and blue yachting pants, there was nothing reassuring in J-P's manner; he seemed capable at best of a spooky kind of good will.

"You know, I have you to thank for a great favor."

"Oh?" Parker shielded his eyes to look at him. "What's that?"

"This woman in Mexico City. I had the idea I could control

her from such a great distance, but I can't. Not even if I was closer, not even if I stood over her *vingt quatres heures par jour.* But you—" Poking the burning tip of the Gaulois at him. "You fucking her right under my nose, *that* makes me see. This is a great favor and a true sign of friendship."

Cautiously Parker replied: "You'd do the same for me."

J-P leaned back again, sighing. "Lupe, my angel, *la belle dame sans merci.*"

A silence fell over the rooftop patio. Together they watched a flock of brown pelicans skim the surface of waves in precise single-file. He hoped his fear wasn't completely obvious, hoped that by continuing to lie still in the recliner this was just another chat between old friends. But there was no getting around it—to arrange a vicious beating and then underwrite the full recovery was J-P's complicated way of saying, All is forgiven.

But nothing's ever forgiven, he thought, and charity equals obligation. Under J-P's wing again he'd be asked sooner or later to do something more dangerous than smuggle money across the border. And when he'd politely decline, he'd be . . . unforgiven.

"This dream I had, maybe it's a sign. Might be a good time to visit the folks back in . . . Wheeling." He tilted his head as casually as possible. "What do you think?"

J-P shot up in the deck chair, flicking away the half-smoked cigarette, and slapped him across the face in the European style, a hand across both cheeks, lightly but not without emphasis.

"Parker, don't worry! The future will take care of itself."

That was when he knew he was getting out.

Later, alone in the room, as late afternoon sounds gave way

to sleepy dusk, a bold strategy came to him. J-P had told him he was entertaining a young woman of recent acquaintance at the five-star French restaurant across the street. So he dressed and went downstairs, hoping to find the front desk unoccupied—it was—and a rack of car keys within easy reach. He knew J-P's taste in automobiles and there they were, keys to a black Porsche 911 he found parked around the corner. Soon he was speeding south on I-5 at the helm of barely containable German-engineered horsepower, a stark contrast to weeks of confined, immobile solitude. On the right a sweep of dark ocean, on the left pale hills dotted with the vaporous lights of empty model homes. In the euphoria of sudden freedom and grand theft auto, he wanted to drive, drive, drive forever; but seeing a sign LAGUNA BEACH NEXT TWO EXITS his euphoria faded, and he realized that proceeding in this vein would be wildly inadvisable. At the next exit he joined a line of summer-evening traffic as it snaked by every art gallery, real-estate office and boutique nail salon on South Coast Highway, parking at the bus station, locating a pay-phone, dialing J-P's home number in Los Angeles. When the answering machine beeped he said, "Hey, man, sorry about how things turned out, but *C'est la vie*, right? Your car's safe and sound at a place of mass transit somewhere on the coast. I'm going out of town for awhile, but next time I'm back I'll be sure to—" A bus honked in the background. "Gotta go, pal, see you around." And hung up, simple as that.

The next bus was leaving for Bakersfield, no place he wanted to go; instead he followed a lively party of three—two guys in silver-gray tuxedos, a much younger girl in a short black dress—into a yuppie bar across the street. The interior featured cascading foliage, Human League and Fine Young Cannibals pounding in wall-to-wall sound. Soon they were buying him drinks, regaling him with tales of drunken debauchery at a wedding reception earlier in the day in Newport Beach; he told a few stories of his own about kidnappings, desert beatings, R&R in a comfortable, undisclosed location—stories no one believed, least of all himself.

After midnight the little band of revelers clustered in the men's room where Raoul—a swarthy man with a Marine-style buzz-cut—laid out lines of a dusty gray powder on the chrome-metal sink. The girl went first, a hungry gleam in her eye as she dove in and out. Parker balked at his turn, but Ike—all skin and bones, a virtual skeleton—urged him on. He leaned over, inhaled the scratchy powder deep in his nose. He looked at the girl, smiling for her own reasons, and said, "Nothing's happening." Then the rush took off the top of his head, like surgical tongs peeling back his scalp and plunging deep inside brain tissue, over and over and over again, never-ending seizures of joy. The others formed a protective cordon and hustled him out of the bar past mocking stares, weird laughter and the unholy baritone of Depeche Mode:

Never again
Is what you swore
The time before

Outside, dazzling neon and deafening street noise combined to drop him on the curb like a sack of rocks. Ike and

Raoul scooped him up with a laugh and deposited him in the back of a waiting gypsy cab.

The air was cool here. A green-glass light bulb such as found in a pool hall dangled overhead. The space had a cave's mildewed smell. Muffled voices came through the ceiling, like voices dropping from clouds. Under the naked light bulb everything was green, the chilly ceramic tiles under his fingers, a wine rack in a narrow alcove, two men in tuxedos slouched against a reinforced stone wall and the girl in a glimmering green dress, laid out against the opposite wall. All of them, Parker included, splayed out in a wine cellar as though knocked off their feet by gale force winds.

The skeleton in the tux lurched to his knees, began crawling toward the wine rack in an alcove in the faux limestone wall. The girl, who had brownish hair over ruby stud earrings, caught Parker looking at her and smiled. Her soft pliable face made him think of bruised fruit.

Raoul pointed to his emaciated green companion, crawling ineffectually toward his destination.

"Ike's in the witness protection program," he said. "The feds back in Trenton busted him for laundering mob money. He turned state's evidence and now nobody knows where he is. Or who."

"State's evidence," Ike laughed or coughed. "That's a good one."

"If the wiseguys ever find him, he's kaput, *finito,* end of story. Won't be enough left over to feed the fish." He smiled at Parker, a grin teetering somewhere between avuncular and crazed. "Let's keep it our little secret, OK? I mean, you can't trust anyone these days. Here we are talking and drinking like gentlemen, but what if I was a hit man or something? What then?"

"It'd be fish-feeding time," Parker said.

"Damn right."

Raoul extended his left arm, held the wrist steady with his right hand, appeared to aim down the barrel of his index finger. The girl laughed. Ike looked up, saw what was happening, and laughed, too.

"Pow," Raoul said, his arm and wrist recoiling.

Ike cried, "No!" and toppled over.

"Got you, you squealing rat bastard."

Groaning, gasping, both hands clasped over his bullet-ridden cummerbund, Ike died in slow-motion inches away from Parker. The girl couldn't stop laughing. Everyone was laughing.

Finally, bottle in hand, Ike resumed his rudderless journey across the wine cellar floor. The light was a pervasive fish-tank green, smoothing his sharp elbows and knees, streamlining him into a shark in formal wear headed—Parker couldn't help noticing—directly for him. In desperation he looked to the girl in the shimmering dress.

"Whose wedding?" he asked.

She looked blank. "What?"

"Who got married today?"

The girl exchanged glances with Ike and Raoul, looks suggesting whole worlds of unthinkable depravity, and giggled. "Me."

Raoul beckoned to her and, smiling vaguely, she slid off her heels and crept across the floor to him. In the oppressive green light he maneuvered her so that she rested her back against his knees. He began massaging her strapless shoulders. The girl closed her eyes and went limp.

"Ummm . . ."

Ike meanwhile came up beside Parker, smelling of garlic and menthol cigarettes. He nodded at the spectacle in front of them. "Disgusting, isn't it? Guy's old enough to be her father."

Yeah, he thought, watching ugly hands roam freely over her body, lingering at the collarbone, edging slightly down again.

"Tell me, cowboy. How're you fixed for cash?"

Parker looked at him. "What?"

"I mean, look at you . . ." Ike indicated the torn windbreaker and day-old stubble on his face. "You don't look exactly flushed with success to me." Nudging him in the ribs: "She's hot, isn't she? Look it how she opens her mouth like that—*there*, just the tip of her little pink tongue. Pretty fucking hot." He leaned closer. "She wants you, cowboy. Told me in the cab."

The girl struggled to look up. "Did I? I can't remember."

"I do," Raoul said, and gently pushed her forward. Firm manicured fingers pressed Parker ahead as well. Ike whispered in his ear, "We like to watch." She slumped or fell in his arms, her lifeless body draped over his shoulders, a warm ripe body impossibly soft to the touch. When he kissed her, the girl came alive, slithering free of the dress, pulling off his clothes, purring eagerly amid a blur of green, heavy-breathing spectators. Now she straddled him, putting his hands on her breasts, nipples rising under his fingertips. With an extravagant sigh she guided him inside, then erupted in a series of convulsions and happy cries, taking him forcibly with her, far from dank green wine cellars and gangsters in tuxedos.

Parker was twenty-eight years old, with nowhere to go but up. So he went home.

9

Not blood, he realized a moment later.

Before that, the sight of so much carnage was alarming and incomprehensible—Eugenia, in a bonnet and frilly black dress like a Prohibition-era vigilante, looming over Mother sprawled across the breakfast table, arms and legs flailing.

"Well?" Now the gory utensil dangled inches from Parker's face. "Do you want some of this, too?"

"Eugenia, put that down."

"Make me, little boy."

Rita swept in, disarmed the old woman, settled her in a chair. With his help she eased Mother off the table and seated her as well; his hands came away smeared with blood, brain tissue and acorn-sized bits of bone matter.

"See?" Mother said. "See what she did to me?"

Steam rising off his fingers. For the first time in all the commotion, he noticed the aroma of garlic and onions.

"Snuck in here like—"

Not blood, he realized.

"—a thief in the night—"

On his shirt, on his shoes, all over the floor: spaghetti sauce.

"—tried to *murder* me!"

"Now now," Rita said, sponging her brow. "It hardly broke the skin."

"No thanks to her!"

Fucking spaghetti sauce, he thought. Mother's attention shifted from the injustice at hand to a closer look at his face. "You shaved that beard off."

"Oh yeah." He kept forgetting. "What do you think?"

"*I* think," Eugenia said, "there's way too much whining and complaining going on. I can't believe my son married such a crybaby."

"That's it—"

Mother shot out of the chair too fast for anyone to stop her. In the process of trying, Parker lost his footing and slid across the scummy floor; Rita, also trying to help, went down with him in a tangle of arms and legs. Nothing stood between the old woman and her stout daughter-in-law's homicidal rage—until Walt appeared. Mother struck him head-on, a prisoner of momentum, bouncing off his torso as though it was a brick wall and landing on the floor alongside her marinara-drenched offspring.

Walt looked down at her, disgusted. "You're a mess."

"Me! What did I do?"

Eugenia poked the tip of her cane in Walt's back. "You tell her, Waldo."

"She's a old woman," Walt said. "Completely harmless."

"Harmless! She cracked me over the head with a steel ladle."

"Tell it to her straight, Waldo."

He swung around, snarling: "The name is *Walt*." Then he lurched from the kitchen and upstairs to his room.

Rain tapped at the window like a gently inquiring neighbor. Parker struggled to his feet, none of his dignity intact, then helped the others. He frowned at Eugenia.

"You know, Mother feeds you and takes care of you. You can't go around hitting her on the head anytime you want."

To which the old woman replied by inflating her cheeks and sticking out her tongue; the sound she made was loud and discourteous. Briefly he too wished to haul back and let her have it.

Again Rita intervened, wagging a finger with far more authority than him. "Eugenia, we're trying very hard to be patient with you."

She wilted in her chair. "Yes, dear."

"But this has to stop *right now*."

"Yes, dear."

Rita's stern finger in the air suggested a wisdom beyond her years, beyond all Parker's exotic misadventures thousands of miles away. She knew how to keep this band of flesh-and-blood lunatics together, day after day, years on end. The gesture, the "gift," the urgent, unquestioning loyalty to family—all this made Rita seem wondrously strange and new to him, not the gangly pre-teen of another time, but a woman with her own secrets and mysteries.

Rita turned, as if pulled by his thoughts. "Would you take Eugenia upstairs? After all this excitement I think she needs a nap."

The old woman allowed him to take her by the elbow and guide her around puddles of red sauce. Behind them at the breakfast table, Mother wept.

"It's the Lord's will," she said. "I must have done something horrible as a child."

Eugenia snickered. "Praise the Lord."

Slow going down the hall; even with his assistance, Eugenia took a long time reaching the stairs. There she gripped the banister and looked up at him.

"Do you think I'm old?" she asked. "I don't think I am."

"Of course not." Gently he shepherded her upward.

"I believe I'll wake up one fine day and it'll be 1912 all over again. It was extremely hot in the summer of 1912."

"As I recall," he said, "August was the hottest month."

"That's right!" She was delighted to be swapping memories. "Remember we went to Popham Beach for corn fritters and sarsaparillas?" She took a single shaky step. "Oh, Boston was so unmercifully hot that summer." Another step. "You couldn't *buy* a breeze on Beacon Hill."

At the top of the landing Eugenia was out of breath; fortunately her bedroom was first on the right, and he could ease her inside and onto the grand four-post bed without much trouble. Settled between the sheets, the old woman beckoned him close. He leaned over, felt hot dry breath like the desert on his face.

"The Ice King," she whispered. "He's coming soon."

"Is that right?"

"It'll be a hard winter, with plenty of ice to pack in sawdust and sell later on. Come July he'll sail down to Patagonia—where, I might add, the natives are simply *frantic* for ice—and trade for all sorts of valuable goods, such as emeralds and indigo and jute." Above the blanket her tiny hands wrestled in joy. "They tell me he has a beautiful mansion in Old Scollay Square. There's a wharf in his name in every port along the Eastern Seaboard."

"When did you see him last?"

Eugenia blinked. "Who?"

"The Ice King."

"1895," she said. "He's about due."

With that, the old woman nodded off, coquettish rapid eye-movements suggesting the matriarch of a once-proud Boston Brahmin clan was chasing rabbits in her sleep. But as he rose from the bed, a hand brittle as rock candy shot out and locked on his wrist.

"Can I trust you? I have to tell someone."

He sighed. "OK."

"It's the soup."

"The soup . . ."

"She put ant-killer in the soup," Eugenia told him. "In the clam chowder, too! I caught her pouring a whole box of that stuff in the sauce. That's why I had to clobber her."

An antique banjo-clock on the night-stand read: 2:15. It seemed in many ways like the longest day of his life.

"But that's a good thing," Parker said. "Ant-killer's good for the circulation, didn't you know that?"

"Really?" She closed her eyes and slept again, freed of a great burden.

His own memories came flooding back—a boy of seven or eight stretched out on this same bed listening while Eugenia sat in the rocker sewing doilies and spinning tales of witch trials and capsized whalers. Out the window he saw that storm clouds had lifted, the immense horizon of snow a blank white slate on which disturbing images of the past few days danced like snowflakes—steel ladles, rotary engines, turtles falling from the sky, a sea of blood-colored spaghetti sauce. Ant-killer! Twelve-gauge shotguns! There was madness in this house. It could no longer be ignored or denied.

His scalp tingled; he felt a prickly sensation in his gut. Was this what duty felt like? Suddenly he knew he wouldn't "take off first chance you get," as Walt predicted. This is my family, he thought. My responsibility.

A fruit bat zipped through the flat afternoon light. Eugenia twitched in her sleep, warm as toast again in 1912.

With renewed purpose he crossed the hall and banged on Walt's door. No answer. From inside came the sound of grinding and drilling. He tried the doorknob: locked. "Hey!" he yelled, banging again.

The door creaked open. Walt's unruly square head poked out. His eyes behind the thick glasses looked cloudy and sad. "Yeah? What do you want?"

"You've got problems," Parker said. "We can talk about it, OK? I'm on your side."

Walt stepped into the hall wearing a brown robe barely

covering frayed white jockey shorts. In his hand was a ball-peen hammer and on his face—lips contorted, cheeks oddly raised—the smile of a murderer.

"See this what I'm holding?" he said. "I think I'm gonna take this thing and split your skull open with it. Then depending on how I feel, I might move on to other parts—your jaw maybe, or how 'bout a kneecap? That's what I think I might do."

Parker stood his ground. "I know what's going on. You want to get out, but you can't."

"Huh?"

"You've got some screwed-up plan to leave with Rita, but you can't. The old man won't let you."

Walt only stared.

"The hell with the old man! I won't let you."

Walt backed into the room, arms spread as if vainly trying to protect the engine block on the floor. "What about you? Why don't *you* just leave?"

I considered it, he thought. But the sight of genuine terror in Walt's face caused his own anger to cool.

"I'm not going anywhere," he said. "Understand? I'm staying right here."

10

When he returned to the kitchen, he saw that the floor had been mopped clean, all the utensils washed and placed in drawers, stove and countertops restored to their usual sheen—all trace of violence gone, as was Rita, the one responsible for cleaning up. He went upstairs in search of her, stopping instead at the door to Burke's study. What about those "documents" Walt had mentioned? Memoirs posing a threat to national security? Or—and this seemed just as likely—the ranting of a madman with a happy trigger-finger. Could they be in here?

He paused, a hand on the doorknob. Look at me, he thought. Home just a few days and already I'm lying, scheming, thinking impure thoughts. Not much to brag about after all this time on my own. The doorknob fumbled open. Add to the list, breaking and entering.

Inside a frosty sunlight hung in the air, mingled with the stale scent of cigar. In one corner, an army cot with regulation bedding; in another, an antique mahogany roll-top desk. On the walls, framed photographs of Burke with congressmen, ambassadors, a gap-toothed secretary of state. He remembered sneaking in here as a kid, staring up at bookshelves lined with inscrutable titles—*Jude the Obscure, Typee, The Influence of Sea Power Upon History*—awed and frightened by knowledge looming overhead like some dust-breathing monster.

"Can I help you, son?"

Burke stood in the hall with a towel around his waist. He'd been shaving or was just about to, his mouth and jaw blurred by a nimbus of white foam. The effect when he smiled was very unsettling.

"No, I was just—" Parker indicated the bookshelves. "Looking for something to read."

Even half-naked, Burke's taut pectorals and stumpy wrestler's legs were more imposing that most people fully clothed. "Good news," he said. "I've been out scouting conditions. We can do the old hunter-gatherer thing anytime you like. Hell, what's wrong with right now? Still got some daylight left. Gives us a chance to stretch our legs."

He said, "Would it make any difference if I said no?"

The old man threw back his bald head and laughed, exposing an obscenely pink palate under all the lathered foam.

"Come on! It'll be fun."

Parker crossed the yard, swaddled in flannel shirt, heavy wool sweater and hand-me-down canvas coat. Knee-high snowdrifts robbed him of much mobility.

A space had been left pried open for him in the barbed-wire

perimeter. He slid the deer rifle through first, though climbing in after it proved a difficult task. Rusted arrow-head barbs snagged the coat, ripped the canvass sleeves. Finally he stood in virgin snow beyond the old stone wall. The sun drained a last-gasp yellow in the dirty sky.

Splat!

A grenade-sized snowball whirling out of nowhere caught him in the forehead; he went down in a patch of velvety snow and stayed there, regaining his senses. Was that laughter he heard rippling through the trees? Yes—there was Burke in black bomber's jacket scrambling in and out of snow-covered spruce woods. Laughing.

Less snow on the ground the farther they got in the woods, at most a light sprinkling on old brush and fallen tree limbs. Light arched through branches, flat and impersonal. A crow squawked at their approach; otherwise, it was quiet.

And cold, much colder than he recalled from childhood—cold that stung your eyes, dried up your mouth, scraped the lining of your lungs. Years spent under the California sun had definitely thinned his blood, and the odd heft of a Winchester .30-.30 in his hands was further disconcerting.

"What're we out here looking for anyway?"

Burke walked ahead of him, his own rifle, a .30-06 close to his side. "Legend has it, a great bull moose roams the countryside, lost during migration to Canada. Nine-point buck, could weigh twelve, fifteen hundred pounds. A mythical creature, perhaps, but I mean to have him."

Parker looked around as if the fabled beast might come

crashing out of the trees at any time. "I'm not shooting any moose," he said.

The old man shrugged, kept on walking.

Biting winds seemed to find every tiny gap in his multi-layered outfit. He felt his upper body stiffening, the snowball wound to his forehead throbbing like an exposed nerve, his ears under the worthless watch cap probably in an early stage of frostbite.

Burke on the other hand appeared invigorated by sub-freezing temperatures, waxing nostalgic as he pushed through snow and underbrush. "Other day I happened to recall something from early childhood—the day my father took us to Wellfleet, to see a finback whale that had washed up on shore. I'll never forget it, the sounds coming from it laid out in the sand. High-pitched, bleating, you know? Like a lamb."

Parker focused less on the story and more on taking one step at a time, carefully following the old man's makeshift trail through an alder thicket, across a frozen stream, through a boulder-clogged gully. The effort to keep up, as exhausting as it was, seemed to keep him moderately warm.

"Well, anyway, the tide swept in as tides always do, covered the finback's blow-hole, and that was the end of that. The good people of Wellfleet hired a boat to haul it off, but a quarter-mile out at sea the hawser snapped and the damn thing sank to the bottom. A few days later it washed ashore again, swelled up from its decomposing gases like a hot-air balloon. Elements set in after that—insects, sea birds, salt wind—left behind a stench that brought tears to the eyes of longshoremen in far-off Barnstable Harbor."

Daylight lingered in a patch of aspen. He felt he'd suffered through the anecdote and had nothing to show for it. "What a bummer for the whale," he said.

Burke trekked on through crusty snow.

They came to a stop where the trail abruptly ended, a narrow outcropping over a ravine. He was grateful for the chance to stop, and for the stainless steel flask that Burke magically produced from inside his jacket and handed over to him. Sour mash whiskey burned his throat, igniting small brush fires in his gut.

"Good stuff," he said, returning the flask.

Burke sat on a long flat rock, taking in the view. "Like Yugoslavia," he said, "winter of '44. Dropping on mountain strongholds far behind enemy lines."

"You mean, like spies?"

"Amateurs, really, all of us from Wild Bill Donovan on down." He drank, then handed back the flask. "Of course, nobody knew what they were doing back then. Guerrilla warfare was a whole new ballgame."

"And this is in the book."

Burke turned, squinted at him. "The book . . ."

"Yeah, the one you're writing—allegedly." He had another long pull, enjoying the whiskey. "Where's it hidden at? I'd love to read a chapter or two sometime." Reckless talk, he knew, but what the hell. "You know, I was just telling Walt how good it feels being home again. Mother says I should've called first, let you know I was coming. But where's the fun in that? I figured, better to just show up on the doorstep."

Suddenly it was crucial that they establish, once and for all, that when the old man aimed and fired the twelve-gauge in the den the day before, he knew exactly what he was doing. "So that's what I did," Parker said. "I just showed up."

Burke's granite profile offered nothing.

"I didn't expect to get *shot at*." He also didn't think he'd been shouting, but crows perched on branches overhead scolded him for the noise.

His stepfather came to his feet, brushing snow off his pants. "Feel better getting that off your chest? Let's go."

Up ahead, the black jacket flitted in and out of barren oak, a voice, it seemed to him, coming from many directions at once.

"—when you lit out for the territories—restless kid—*itchy*—"

How long had have we been walking? he thought. Hours, days? Soon nightfall would plunge them into primal darkness, each with a loaded deer rifle in his hands. The prospect held no joy in it.

"It had a lot to do with you," he told the bobbing, weaving voice.

"Oh?"

"Moving us way the hell out here, for one thing. Making it sound like we'd get eaten alive the minute we stepped out of the house." A chuckle wafted from the trees. "Other kids got bedtime stories. We got food riots in Cairo, beggars starving to death in India—and don't forget the swarming hordes of Red Chinese."

At first no response from the spectral presence, confusing

him as to which way to turn. Then, on his right:

"—thought you'd benefit from my vast overseas experience—"

On his left:

"—come scurrying home with your tail between your legs—"

On his right again:

"—don't say I didn't warn you—"

Wind swept up off the forest floor and into Parker's face. "I left 'cause I wasn't a kid anymore, and I sure as hell wasn't going to take *your* word for it—"

A fallen tree trunk lay on the path, but he never saw it. He tripped and fell in a bed of dry pine needles, losing hold of the rifle and twisting his ankle in the process.

"Owwww—!"

The black jacket materialized in front of him. "And?"

Rubbing his ankle, grimacing. "And *what?*"

"Is the great teeming planet everything I said it would be?"

"No!" Parker cried. "I mean, yes. Maybe. I don't know."

Burke faded off into the trees, a ghost again.

Trudging on, farther and farther. Where are we? he wondered. How far from home? A gauzy dusk blunted sharp edges around him; more than once he swerved at the last minute to avoid low-hanging branches, coming down hard each time on his tender ankle. He was convinced by now there weren't any moose out here, legendary or otherwise; this ridiculous forced march was meant to show Burke's physical mastery over the lean, irrelevantly tanned young man currently hobbling in the snow behind him like a prisoner of war.

"So I came home unannounced," he said. "Big deal."

An ambivalent grunt up ahead.

"The question is, what's going on *here*? How come Walt's pissed off all the time and Rita's acting nervous and scared—since when did Mother get religion? How come nobody's . . ." He stumbled on the word.

"What?"

" . . . happy."

Laughter spilled out of the arboreal gloom. "Happy? Is that what's bothering you? We're not one big happy family?"

"Yeah," Parker said, flummoxed by the entire exchange. He found Burke waiting for him in a small clearing.

"Happy, unhappy, right, wrong. It never ceases to amaze me," he said, "the moral authority of youth. When did society relinquish control and put *you* in charge of everyone's good conduct? What the hell do you know about anything?"

"There was a time when you were happy," Parker said. "You got too goddamn old to remember."

"I was happy doing what I believed in. Can you say the same?"

In fact, he couldn't; now he raised the deer rifle, aiming this way and that. "Where's the moose? Let's shoot us some moose."

"Son, allow me an observation."

"Yeah, sure."

"You see how your mother's got her eye peeled for the heavenly plan, the grand scheme of things—and so, I fear, do you. You say you're not a kid anymore? Then let me be clear:

You're barking up the wrong tree!" Gusts of white-hot vapor spilled from his mouth. "There isn't any pay-off, only muddling through life as we've always muddled through, stupid, self-absorbed, heedless of tomorrow. We've become a nation bloated on greed, struck dumb by our own mindless power. We're *beached,* son. Like that finback whale. Just waiting for the next tide to wash in over us."

Parker looked up at the heavy gray sky, wondering if he'd ever be free of this man.

"Things were different in my day," the old man went on. "We didn't equivocate, we took *action*. As for bedtime stories and the like . . . I guess I wasn't cut out for weeding the tomato patch and changing diapers in the first place."

It was as great an admission of parental shortcomings as he remembered hearing; but with Burke you could never be sure. "It's a little late to be saying this now."

"Oh, I'm not apologizing. I'll go to my grave knowing I did the very best I could for my family."

The appalling injustice of this remark took Parker's breath away; when it came back, his teeth were chattering. "Maybe you could've d-d-done better! It's a mess—ant-killer in the soup, Walt building a plane to fly to Easter Island—"

"My theory is brain damage."

"He says he's t-t-taking Rita."

After a lengthy pause, Burke let out a hearty laugh; surprised, Parker joined in. The echo in the woods sounded very hollow.

"Too bad about Walt," his stepfather said. "In any case, I've seen what the world can do to your spirits. I won't have my daughter sullied by such things. Rita stays here."

"Even if she d-d-doesn't want to—"

"She leaves," Burke said, "over my d-d-dead body."

Male rage, ugly and thuggish, passed between them.

Something rustled in a pile of dead brush several yards away. In the time it took Parker to register the sound, Burke pivoted in a half-crouch and raised the .30-06 to eye-level, flicking the safety and taking aim at what looked like an unbroken wall of pine. Then he saw a flash of white-tail, a blur of tawny hide.

Burke fired.

There was a roar close to his ear. Branches shattered, dark winged creatures bursting like shrapnel in the air. The deer escaped in the woods, unharmed.

Not so Parker, on his knees now in the snow, hands over his ringing ears. The last time a weapon had been discharged in his presence, he'd quivered for his life. *That* wouldn't happen again. Slowly he came to his feet, took hold of the Winchester he'd propped against a tree and shoved the barrel in the small of his stepfather's back.

"Here's your d-d-dead body . . ."

Burke raised his hands casually, an unworried mugging victim. "Son, let me stop you right there."

"Huh?"

"Truth is, no one gives a rat's ass for your thoughts on the matter."

"Shut up!" Whatever Parker hoped from this confrontation, he wasn't getting it. He poked the rifle deeper in Burke's spine, causing him to lurch in the snow; at no time did he display anything like duress. "C-c-come on! Let's see what sc-scared really looks like—"

For a long moment, it seemed, he'd persuaded both of them that he was capable of anything. The moment passed. Burke turned to face him, his eyebrows lightly frosted, nostrils tinged with ice.

"Don't worry, son. We'll get that buck next time."

And headed off the direction they'd come, leading into a cluster of pine and beyond. Parker stayed in the clearing, a useless grip on the rifle—worse than useless, since he had a finger on the trigger and didn't shoot. Most painful of all, picturing a huge blinking scoreboard where points were tallied in neon stadium lights, points for him, points for the old man, for all eternity. This stupid little outburst, he knew, had cost him plenty.

Without Burke's footprints to follow, he might have been lost in the woods forever; as it was, the path was clear enough and he eventually straggled home, soon after nightfall. He left his boots and the rifle in the hall closet, went upstairs to change into dry clothes. A quick glimpse in other bedrooms—all empty—then downstairs to the living room where someone had thoughtfully left a fire burning in the fireplace. He sat on the hearth close to the flames, his body craving all the heat it could find, to warm icy skin and relieve a deeper, subcutaneous cold.

"I can't hear!"

Startled, he nearly toppled into the fireplace. It was Eugenia, seated in the wing chair behind him, clutching her shawl and pointing urgently at the TV—grainy underwater footage of sharks, great whites devouring lesser fish.

"I can't hear!" she cried. "I think I've gone deaf!"

"Hold on . . ." He raised the volume on a Frenchman's reedy voice-over. "How's that?"

"Switch it!"

"What?"

"Switch channels! I can't abide that Jack Coo-Stow fellow."

A vast weariness descended as he checked random programming for her, the results of an afternoon spent braving the elements for no reason, as well as lingering shame over his own bad behavior. Maybe he was blending in better than he thought. He pictured himself growing old in this house, a decrepit creature missing hair and a mouthful of teeth, wandering the drafty halls alone. The last sorry one left.

"Mr. Ed! Leave that on."

Settled in the armchair, Parker dozed off to the gentle sparks of fire, canned music and applause, the old woman's high-pitched laughter. Sometime later he woke to the themesong from "Bonanza." Eugenia sat slouched over in the wing chair, eyes closed, deeply puckered lips open; the longer he stared the less she appeared to be breathing. In a panic he seized her wrist and shook it. "Save the estate!" she cried, and promptly returned to sleep.

Other voices trailed in—real ones, not voices on TV—and he forced himself up to investigate, a simple task that inflamed aching muscles in his arms and legs, jump-started fresh pain in his ankle. The voices came from across the hall. He stopped outside the door to the den, listening.

" . . . a lifetime spent keeping my enemies at bay . . ."

"Yes, Daddy."

" And here they are . . ."

"No, it's OK—"

"In my very own home."

Meaning me, Parker thought. Because the den was poorly lit—a student lamp casting a bleak, after-hours glow over ceiling beams and pine-paneled walls—he could slip inside unseen. Burke stood by the pool table in a wine-dark turtleneck sweater; his head was bowed, shoulders hunched, a man rendered senseless with grief.

And Rita in a peasant dress standing beside him, attempting for some unfathomable reason to comfort him.

"We're safe, Daddy, as long as we stick together."

"No," he told her, "we'll never be safe."

For Parker, an amazing sight—the patriarch, the leader, the household dictator, reduced to tears.

"Come here," Burke said, holding out his arms.

Watching her succumb to his embrace, Parker thought: How long has *this* shit been going on? Under different circumstances it should have been *him* alone somewhere with her, a summer field perhaps, lying together in a blaze of goldenrod. Instead, Burke's thick pulpy fingers circled her waist.

Too much for him, he stepped out of the shadows. "Enemies everywhere," he said.

She jerked away, surprised, but the old man held on, all sadness and mania gone, replaced by a familiar hard-eyed gaze and look of disgust. He seemed to address Rita while staring across the pool table at Parker.

"Sometimes," Burke said, "when a young man leaves home,

a strange thing happens. If he should succeed in life as, say, Parker has, then it's a triumph of his own making, no tip of the hat to the old folks at home." With his free hand he tipped an imaginary hat. "If on the other hand our young man washes out, fails in his endeavors, the cause no doubt will be traced back to childhood—abuse, neglect, whatever. Either way, the family is the scapegoat."

Watching her squirm, Parker wished he hadn't put the deer rifle away. "Who're we talking to now?" he asked. "The paranoid super-patriot or whacked-out family man?"

Burke grinned. "Are those my only choices?"

"Stop making speeches and let her go."

"Pardon me?"

"Get your fucking hands off her."

Rita stood paralyzed, afraid to look at either of them. Burke assumed a thoughtful expression, as if weighing the pros and cons of Parker's demands. When he released her at last, Rita danced away, breathless, in the shadows of a rack of cue-sticks on the wall.

"I don't recall you being this assertive," Burke said. "In the old days you'd never have spoken to your father like that."

He answered, through gritted teeth: "You're not my father."

"Well, in a manner of speaking—"

What happened next happened fast, or seemed to. Parker took a cue-stick off the wall and, gripping it like a big-league batter, swung for the stands against exposed chimney bricks and snapped it in half. In a kind of trance he took a step forward and plunged the jagged tip in his stepfather's chest. Screams.

Blood splashing from punctured arteries. Burke writhing on the floor with the butt-end of a cue-stick jutting from his turtleneck. *In a manner of speaking!*

"No," Parker heard a distant voice saying, "not here . . ."

He opened his eyes. Burke stood in front of him, smiling and unscathed. But Rita shrank away, as if she'd seen the horrible things he'd only imagined doing.

"How could you?" There were tears in her eyes. "How could you think such things?"

"Rita, wait—"

"Not here, not in this house."

"Listen to me—"

"No!"

The two men listened to the slap of her bare feet running upstairs, then a bedroom door banging shut and thick oppressive silence. Burke rummaged inside the liquor cabinet in search of cigars, while he took the time to collect his thoughts, purge himself of all homicidal fantasies. But the sawed-off cue-stick had been so *real*. He asked: "Is there a will? Last will and testament?"

"Aha!" Burke located a box of panatelas and lit one with obvious satisfaction. "What you see before you is the extent of my worldly belongings."

"Really? Nothing saved up for a rainy day?"

Burke chomped on the cigar. "State your business. One thing I can't stand, it's young people spouting innuendo."

"Rumors, is all. Ugly rumors." He counted off seconds in his head. "Something about a fortune in government bribe money."

No mistaking it this time; a nerve had been struck. Parker saw the frown, the brief but discernible twitch of the left eyebrow. He savored the victory.

It was short-lived. The front door opened, sending a small blizzard down the hall. Heavy feet tramping toward them in the den. Now what? he thought. Mother appeared in the door wearing a shiny yellow raincoat. Her face was dripping, her graying hair plastered in streaks to her forehead. Even from where he stood, the freakish intensity in her eyes was alarming. When she spoke however, her voice was oddly calm.

"It's raining cats and dogs out there."

Burke sighed, parted the curtains for a look outside.

"Speaking of dogs, that wretched beast of yours threw up in the bathroom again. The third time this week! When will you put that poor thing out of its misery?"

"Rain's going to let up soon," Burke said, still looking outside. "Then we'll see some *real* snow."

For Mother, apparently, this was the last straw; she stormed into the den, spraying rain and slush in Parker's face, and took up a hostile stance behind her husband.

"I know you can hear me, even when you act like I'm not here. Look! Look!" Waving yellow day-glow sleeves like a demented crossing guard. "I'm right here!"

"Yes," he said, turning at last, "there you are. There you always have been. And who pray tell will put me out of *my* misery?"

She slapped him, the sound echoing off walls and making Parker flinch. Burke merely stooped to retrieve his fallen cigar; when he stood again, the others saw what was on his face—or wasn't, no rage, no urge to strike back, just a dull empty stare. Mother collapsed in the armchair, crying bitterly. Burke waved away a cloud of cherry tobacco smoke to show him a helpless smile, as if to say, *We're not so different, you and me. We happen to be the kind of man who makes women weep.* The tiny kernel of truth—the slightest possibility that they had anything in common—drove him back to visions of murder, cue-sticks replaced by machete, blow-torch, poison arrow.

Too late. He'd had the opportunity hours ago in the deep woods and squandered it away. The only thing to do was help Mother leave with some dignity. He guided her out of the chair, across the room under Burke's indifferent gaze. As they passed by he said, "Watch your back, old man." It was all he trusted himself to say.

11

Hours later, secluded in his room, Parker was glad there'd been no family dinner. He knew he couldn't have handled it.

Shadows slithered over a washed-out Navajo blanket warming his knees. Burke's gloating smile still haunted him—*not so different, you and me*—the latest in a long series of angry stand-offs in which Parker was usually first to back down. The old man needled Walt through childhood; even singling Rita out for praise was a form of abuse. He'd crashed through their lives like a rogue elephant, leaving nothing behind but mangled, trod-upon souls.

He decided he was hungry after all. While the family slept he went downstairs in a borrowed robe and slippers, finding his way in the dark like he did as a child. Walls cool to the touch, the silence of furniture. The refrigerator held nothing appealing, but rooting around in the cupboards he found—behind two cans of stewed tomatoes and a box of Quaker Oats—what he didn't know he was looking for: Crown Royal whiskey, a bottle three-quarters full.

He sat at the breakfast table, glass and bottle in hand. Outside, snow rolled like plush Berber carpeting all the way to the low stone wall. Pines jutted into a night sky clouded with stars. He realized he'd been at it pretty much all day, from beer at noon in the Bay State Bar & Grill to sour mash from a flask during a mini-polar expedition, drinking now from someone's hidden stash, alone, after midnight. Images of the disastrous hunting trip—including a snowball to the head!—left the taste of whiskey brackish and vinegary on his tongue. Quickly he poured another.

A long moment passed. All was well and quiet, the house felt settled in for the night. Then a furry, heat-producing object brushing against his pajama leg caused him to bolt from the chair—Ajax, panting, wagging his tail, looking up with big brown eyes, as if to say: *Got something for me?* Parker shoved him away with his foot. "Bad dog." Ajax sneezed across his slipper and curled up on the floor.

"I see you've discovered my little secret."

A large pineapple-shaped shadow appeared in the doorway. It was Mother, in a mouse-brown winter coat and sensible black pumps.

"*Our* little secret." He found a glass and invited her to join him. "How come you're all dressed up?"

"Am I?" Mother said, touching her hair. "It's nothing, really." She wore a fair amount of make-up, and carefully combed strands of hair obscured most of the bandage on the side of her head.

"Want to hear what me and Burke did today?"

"Of course," she said, in a way suggesting the opposite. "What did you do today?"

"We went hunting!"

"Oh dear."

"It's OK. We didn't shoot anything."

Mother held her glass up to the light, admiring the gold liquid inside. "They make this stuff up in the Yukon somewhere, did you know that?"

" . . . No."

Together they stared in mute fascination at the Crown Royal label on the bottle. Ajax in the corner grumbled in his sleep.

"She's a good girl," Mother said. "Never could complain about her."

"Who?"

"Rita, of course. Why she's taken to staying on here is utterly beyond me. You and Walt, on the other hand, that's a different story. I believe any objective person would've called you a pair of monsters."

"C'mon," he said with a frightened laugh. "We weren't that bad."

"I remember one morning, the two of you were kids, I happened to be washing dishes at the sink, I looked up and there was smoke rising from the back yard. Good Lord, I thought. *Fire.* I rushed outside and what do I find but Walt snagged up on the clothesline by his shirt collar, dangling over a pile of blazing tinder—and *you* dancing around, whooping it up like a little Indian chief!" She laughed, quick bursts followed by an all-encompassing sigh. "To this day I have no idea what got into you."

"Mother," he said sternly, "that never happened."

"It certainly did. I remember as if it was yesterday."

Out the window, clouds scurried past as if late for an appointment. "What about boyfriends?" he asked.

"Boyfriends?"

"Does Rita have any?"

Mother drained her glass and set it on the table. "There was a boyfriend once, nice young man from down by Great Barrington. Came around a good six months or so. They were in love, I suppose, though these days it's so hard to tell. I see young people in town holding hands and all I can think is, What about thirty years from now? Of course, that didn't occur to me at *their* age."

"The boyfriend . . ."

"Yes, very nice. Rita hinted that marriage might be in the offing. Then one night Burke cornered the boy in the den and grilled him for hours. Who are you? Where are you from? A real third-degree. Jammed his shotgun in the poor boy's face yelling, You can't stop me! I can write anything I want!"

He felt instant affinity with the harassed young suitor, no doubt sharing the same hard-earned insights about yourself experienced at point-blank range. But to Mother his lack of response must have seemed vacant and empty-headed.

"The *book*," she huffed. "Really, Parker, you weren't always this thick between the ears."

"Sorry . . ."

Tapping her ring finger against the glass: another, please. "Don't you see? Burke claimed the boy was seeing Rita only in order to spy on *him*. But it wasn't the government. The government had nothing to do with it. He didn't want anyone near his precious daughter. In any case, that's the last we saw of the boy from Great Barrington."

The grandfather clock chimed twice in the dining room. Two a.m., he thought, and I'm drinking with a woman with a bandage on her head. Clouds enveloped the moon like a pillow lowered over a face. "Tell me about my father."

"Your father . . ." Mother paused to refill their drinks with a bartender's blank efficiency. "He was a lifelong Rotarian. He wore a size ten-and-a-half shoe. Cats made him nervous and he was very fond of lemon meringue pie."

Facts, facts, a goddamn mountain of facts. He wanted more. "More," he said.

"There *is* something else." Tilting her head, she giggled like a schoolgirl. "Maybe I shouldn't say . . ."

"Go ahead. Say."

"It has to do with how he died."

"What about it?" He felt abruptly defensive. "He drowned in a swimming pool. Some guy jumped off the high-dive and landed on his head."

"Turns out, your father had a bad heart," she said, with an air of long-standing grievance, "though *I* was never informed of it."

"A heart attack? In the swimming pool?"

In confusion he watched the clouds slowly dissolve, exposing the pinched features of the moon gasping for air. Mother reached across the table and flicked his ear.

"Are you listening to me?"

"Yeah," he said, rubbing his ear. "Sure."

"There was no swimming pool. On June tenth, 1954, the angel of death swooped down on the Howard Johnson's Motor Lodge outside Arlington, Virginia, and took your father away. One minute he was fine. The next minute, his heart folded up like a circus tent and he was gone."

Wind rattled the back door. Ajax snorted awake, lifting his snout to sample the air for menace, and dropped back to sleep again.

"Well," he said finally. "Sounds like the best way to go."

Mother giggled again.

"In his sleep, right? He died in his sleep?"

"Not exactly."

His throat was parched, he needed water bad. All he had to do was come to his feet and walk to the sink for a glass of water. He got as far as standing; then the surface of earth in the form of rock-hard linoleum came rushing up to greet him. He took it on the chin, sprawled out on the floor.

Mother looked down, apparently unmoved. "Yes, the Lord works in mysterious ways," she said, "but just once, just one time, I'd sure like a clear rational explanation for things."

After his head stopped spinning, Parker agreed. "That would be nice."

Somehow they ended up in the living room, Mother seated more or less upright on the sofa, Parker at her feet in a horizontal slump. Moonlight through the bay window sparkled studs on Ajax's collar, where the dog lay sleeping near the radiator. The whiskey bottle on the coffee table was only moments ago dancing in the air, he was sure of it.

"It wasn't always like this," Mother said, "life under a tyrant's yoke, crazy old woman sneaking around the house. The man I met twenty-one years ago at the Egyptian embassy was kind and gentle—that's what impressed me, how such a big bear-like man could be so tidy, so courteous. A *diplomat,* of all things."

With apparently complete motor control, she poured whiskey in both glasses. He waited; a few extra minutes' wait wouldn't hurt his chances of actually holding onto the thing.

"Something happened after we moved out here. He stayed by himself, went hunting in the woods for days. Couldn't adapt to the notion of having a family." She gave Parker a steady, appraising look. "You might as well know, we don't sleep together anymore. Haven't for quite some time."

"Whoa, hey —"

"When I joined hands in holy matrimony with Burke Sullivan, it was till death do us part. Now *that's* the part that scares me most."

He crawled to the edge of the coffee table, stared hard at the glass. Don't give me any trouble, he thought.

"It never made sense, how a man like your father could be cut down in his prime, while a mean spiteful woman lives to be a hundred. Of course," she added dejectedly, "I never did anything about it."

Where was this going? "OK . . ."

"But when you showed up, that's when it hit me. If somebody doesn't take some kind of action soon, the old witch will outlive us all. That's when I decided—no more fantasies."

Finally mastering the necessary eye-hand coordination, he raised the glass aloft. "To no more fantasies."

"Keep in mind," Mother continued, "I was trying to make the whole thing quick and painless—I still have *some* heart. So last night before we sat down to dinner I secretly laced the—"

"Wait!" he cried, laughing. "I know this one."

"What do you know?"

"Ant-killer! In the clam chowder!"

"No—what? It was—Parker, stop laughing!—Phenobarbital, what the doctor gave me for my insomnia."

But he couldn't stop laughing. "Insomnia! You can't sleep!"

"Who can, with all this craziness going on?"

His scatterbrained merriment was infectious, Mother laughing, too. The old dog looked up, mildly curious about the guffawing bipeds on the sofa. Parker screwed up his face and went into a rendition of Eugenia's pedigree whine: "I don't *like* clam chowder."

"It tastes funny," Mother added in the same affronted tone, and collapsed with him in a fit of laughter.

When they came apart—catching their breath, wiping away tears—Mother went to her purse for a compact to rearrange herself. Hilarity dwindled off into uncomfortable silence, broken finally by the sound of a distant car engine.

"I don't know," he said. "This must break a whole bunch of commandments."

Mother took this to impugn her faith. "You saw what that old crone tried to do to me in the kitchen? Am I supposed to wait around like some witless fool and let her finish me off?"

"I guess not . . ."

"You guess not!"

This isn't family, he thought. This is war. "What if . . . What if *he's* the one who wasn't around anymore? What if we could talk him into leaving and taking Eugenia with him?"

"Life would much simpler, I suppose, and we'd all live happily after." One last look in the compact mirror and Mother snapped it shut. "The problem is, this is Burke Sullivan's house and we are Burke Sullivan's family. He's not about to be persuaded otherwise."

A car was steadily drawing closer.

"That being the case, we've all had to make some adjustments."

Outside, tires eased across gravel. Climbing apelike onto the sofa, he looked out the window at a black-and-white cruiser pulling into the driveway, COUNTY SHERIFF'S OFFICE emblazoned on the side. Mother stood, a bit shakily, and walked to the front door.

"Well? Do I look all right?"

"All right for what?"

The gaze she bestowed on her perplexed son was not unsympathetic. "I know I can count on you, for whatever needs doing."

At first he lost sight of her as she left the house; then she reappeared pushing through ankle-deep snow, crossing before low-beam headlights, opening the passenger door and getting inside. Briefly, two heads merged behind the snow-splattered windshield. Then the cruiser backed out of the drive and swung west on the country road.

Ajax barked again, too late to influence events, and with rare puppyish glee hopped up on the sofa beside Parker. Together, man and dog looked out at the newly restored stillness of the winter night, a postcard version of snowy New England countryside just the way, he imagined, God intended. Licking sounds close to his ear: Ajax lapping at condensation on the window. Moments later he joined in, licking in rhythm with the aged canine, savoring for himself the sting of cold glass on his tongue.

12

In the dream he is running. Moonlight splinters against tree trunks like a hail of gunfire. At the edge of the woods he comes to a frozen lake, a flat table of ice stretching for miles. Closer in, funnels of wind and snow whirl across the surface, wisps with limbs and heads, like ghosts dancing under the stars. He's running for the ghosts when the ice cracks beneath him.

A knock at the door woke him to a sickly gray light. He was still wearing the bathrobe and slippers from the night before, but had no memory of climbing the stairs or getting into bed. Another knock. He sat up, groaning. Rita had been in his dreams.

"I did it! I finished!"

This morning, the range and depth of his ailments made him feel twice his age. Bruised joints, swollen ankle, industrial-strength hangover. And the sight of Walt deliriously happy in the doorway did nothing to help. His overalls were drenched in black grease, in fact he looked covered in it from head to toe, grease, oil, other petroleum by-products. His hair slimy and matted with it, his face smeared as if for jungle warfare. Staring out at the world through oily wire-rim glasses.

Parker rubbed his unbelieving eyes. "What time is it?"

"Noon—what, you just wake up?" Normally this would be the worst kind of slacking off, but today Walt's bright mood was imperturbable. "Did you hear what I said? I *finished*."

"Congratulations. Get the maid to hose you down, OK?"

"Wanna see? C'mon, take a look."

"Maybe later."

"No." He dropped a hand on the bathrobe sleeve and Parker recoiled too late, instantly smelling like a garage mechanic. "Right now."

First glance inside Walt's bedroom showed the usual mess: work boots and balled-up dungarees on the floor, a wasp's nest of drill bits and socket wrenches. The familiar rotary engine sat on a patch of tarpaulin, safe behind a phalanx of empty motor oil cans.

"Were you planning to sleep all day?" Rita asked.

She sat on the edge of the unmade bed in a coral-colored dress, black hair spread over her shoulders.

"Not *all* day," he said.

"*This*." Walt pointed at the engine like a teacher impatient with class. "I rewired the ignition, calibrated the timing, screwed in the cylinder heads. She's ready to go in two, maybe three days at most."

He felt Rita's eyes on him, waiting, hoping he'd play along with this nonsense. The engine looked no different than before, though clearly that was the wrong thing to say; he said it anyway.

"Looks the same to me."

"The same? What're you talking about?" Walt cried. "With a engine like this, a cross-country cruiser can reach sixteen thousand feet in no time, V-max at a hundred-and-thirty per—" Flapping his grease-stained arms to illustrate the concept of flight. "More, if you're red-lining!"

Parker looked at the glossy photos tacked to the wall—swaying palms, giant stone heads. "And go where? Easter Island?"

"That's *Rapa Nui,*" she said.

He turned on her, suddenly annoyed. "Are you going too? Did you help Walt calibrate the timing?"

Rita's bold smile froze, a cautionary shadow passing over her face. Walt didn't notice. He paced the floor, rubbing sticky black hands together, choosing this moment to divulge his previously-secret itinerary—five hundred miles at a time, the *Traveler*'s maximum fuel capacity—from a landing strip outside Springfield, south along the Carolina coast down into Florida, a skip and a jump across the Gulf of Mexico, south again over Columbia, Ecuador, Peru. Brief stop-over in Santiago to rest and refuel, then the last long journey across the South Pacific.

"May take awhile," he admitted, "but we'll get there."

Rita smoothed her dress and smiled at Parker. "Did you know the biggest statue on the island weighs thirty tons? It's called *Te-Piko-Te-Kura.*"

"*Te-Piko-Te-Kura,*" Walt, pacing, repeated aloud.

"Six hundred statues face inland, all except *Los Siete Monos*—the Seven Monkeys."

"*Rapa Nui. Los Siete Monos.*"

"They face out to sea."

She jumped off the bed and dashed to the hallway, peering both ways before joining them near the engine. The breeze of her dress passing by, her easy agility, left him light-headed.

"I know," she said. "Let's invite Parker along."

Walt's eyes blurred to the dingy shade of his overalls. "Uh-uh. There's room just for two."

"But you can fix that, right?"

"No. Takes too long."

"We can wait."

"*No,*" Walt said. "No waiting. Just you and me."

Parker felt like something haggled over in a flea market. "Who says I *want* to go?" But there it was in his head—hot sand under his feet, flesh burned to a crisp by equatorial sunlight. I do, he thought. I want to go.

"OK," he said, "there's the engine. What about the rest—or is that made up, too, like all the other stuff?"

Walt bristled. "What stuff?"

"The bribes and pay-offs and CIA—"

"I told you! I saw the documents!"

"Are they in code, Walt? Invisible ink?"

"That's enough," Rita said, pushing Walt to the door. "Go clean up. We'll be late for class."

"Ain't no goddamn code," Walt grumbled on his way out.

Alone with her, Parker allowed himself free rein to last night's dream—ghost-girls twirling across ice—knowing all the time she could read his thoughts as he had them.

"Can you do that all the time?"

"Do what?"

"You know—read minds."

"I don't *read* anything," she said. "I see pictures of things. But not all the time and only with some people."

"Like me."

"Not all the time."

He indicated the engine block at their feet. "What about that?"

"If you're asking, have I seen a plane—no, I haven't."

"Then you don't really believe he—"

"Walt believes!" Her green eyes flashing at him. "Isn't that the most important thing?"

Maybe so, he thought. The bathroom shower came on down the hall. He tried a different approach. "You know, if you want to get away, we can do a lot better than some lousy desert island."

Rita frowned, a bit curious. "Like where?"

"Anywhere. How about Paris? Or Rome? How about Rio de Janeiro?" He waved his arms in a Walt-like surge of euphoria, lacking any basis in reality but no less heartfelt for it. "Mardi Gras in Rio! Let's do it! Let's go!"

For a moment this seemed to catch her attention. He could feel her longing for better days. Down the hall, Walt was singing in the shower, a lively out-of-tune rendition of "Camptown Races." That—and the inconsolable hoot of a barn owl outside—suddenly drained all life from her. She went to the window, looking pale and despondent.

"I don't know why this is happening, why we're all acting so . . ."

From down the hall: "*Camptown racetrack five miles long—*"

"Crazy?" he said.

"I guess it looks that way. But it's different inside."

"Inside?"

"*—doo dah, doo dah—*"

"You're not here. You're not *inside* anymore."

In spite of everything, this stung him.

"Walt used to mope around," she said, "never knew what to do with himself. Then Doctor Trunk hired him to work on his car. Soon he got all excited about wingspan and climbing altitude and—"

"Easter Island."

"But at least he was happy! Why should anyone spoil that for him?"

"*Bet mah money on de bob-tail nag—*"

"Why should *you?*"

"*Somebody bet on de bay—*"

Things change, he thought. What's the point of coming home in the first place if things don't change? In the wake of her sadness he felt heroic, a knight in shining armor. In his head he told her, *You've changed. The others are beyond saving.* Cupping her sad face in his hands, Parker kissed her.

There was instinctive resistance, muscles going taut in her arms; just as quickly she relented and responded, with a long urgent kiss that ended up startling them both. When they came apart he felt her hot dry breath on his face, a taste of strawberry on her tongue.

Footsteps thudded down the hall. She stepped away, wiping the back of her hand across her mouth in a feral manner.

"What's goin' on?"

Parker sneered at his brother in the doorway, the sprinkling of blonde hair on his winter-white chest, the damp ragged towel wrapped around his waist. "There's one way to prove what you're saying."

Walt squinted around the room through fogged-in glasses. "Huh? What?"

"Let's see the documents."

Off came the glasses, which he scoured frantically with the end of the towel. "I told you, the money got paid in a long time ago. He hid it somewhere nobody can get at it."

"Where?"

Walt calmly replaced the glasses, took a deep breath and shouted in his face. "Secret bank account! Just like I been telling you! Pay attention!"

"No," Parker said just as calmly. "Where are the documents?"

Walt pointed at the study door across the hall.

"OK, let's go."

"Uh-uh. Nobody allowed. Trespassers will be shot."

Rita hung back, unwilling to commit to either camp.

"Can't you see Walt has problems?" he asked her. "He needs our help."

"Problems!" Walt stomped into the walk-in closet, thrashing among clothes inside. Leaving Parker to face her wrath.

"Why are you doing this? Why are you saying these horrible things?"

"To make a point."

"What point?"

"They're all beyond saving."

Walt burst out from the closet in fresh overalls, taking Rita by the arm and pulling her to the door. She looked back long enough for him to see that the pictures he carried in his head—swaying palms, diamond-white beaches—were in her head, too.

Having gone this far, he had no choice but to sneak inside the study. There was the army cot and mahogany roll-top desk, the framed pictures on the wall of Burke alongside white-haired captains of industry. Pungent, ingrained aroma of cigar hanging in the air.

The desk surface was awash in wadded-up bits of paper, nearly engulfing the black rotary-dial telephone and the base of the goose-neck lamp—notes written in a hurried scrawl, like cryptic fortune cookies from the old man's past. "Berlin '45, pissing in the *Fuhrerbunker*" and "Tehran '54, bringing back the Peacock Throne." Other notes included rudimentary arithmetic, sketches of castle-and-moat formations, a parade of angry-looking stick figures racing up and down the page.

No sign of any "documents."

The top desk drawer held a thermometer, passport, referee's whistle, two rolls of Buffalo head nickels, a crumpled brown fedora, and a penlight shaped like a surgeon's scalpel. In the middle drawer a tax ledger bulging with figures; Parker was no CPA, but he guessed where there's smoke, there's fire. Anxious to find ironclad proof of his stepfather's misdeeds, he yanked too hard on the wooden pull and the bottom drawer slid out completely, landing with a thud. Inside, an ivory-handled .45

sat on a sheaf of manila folders.

In the moments that followed he heard no voices or footsteps, nothing except a faint erratic scratching coming from inside the attic; it faded in and out, arrhythmic, suggesting life but something not quite human. Armed with the scalpel-penlight he entered the attic, groping past boxes of old shoes, clothing in mothballs, other ambiguous family artifacts better left unseen. Rafters slanted downward to a corner in the attic, leaving no space to walk upright. The air was dark and musty, smelling like soured milk.

In pursuit of the scratching he crouched and waddled across ceiling beams roughly three feet apart. His breath came in short bursts. His heart banged in his chest.

Now he lay stretched out on a cross-hatched beam peering down into the bowels of the house. A square object rested a few feet below on a narrow plank nailed between posts. He could reach it only by pressing the side of his face into foam insulation, the stink of rotting fluff deep inside his nose, taking hold of a metal handle and slowly hauling it up.

In the thin beam of the scalpel-light was an aluminum strongbox with a complex array of hasps and hinges, the brass padlock on the latch hanging open. Why not? Who'd think to come looking for something here? Raising the lid he trained the light on its contents—a thick stage of typewritten pages, secured with baling twine. On top:

Our Flag Was Still There

By Burke Sullivan, Lt. Col. U.S. Army (ret.)

Underneath the stack of pages, another surprise: rows of neat, densely-packed currency in high denominations, more in fact than he'd expected to ever see in his lifetime. Oddly, though, his interest in the manuscript was stronger, enough so he failed to notice the scratching sound had stopped. So there *was* a book! But the twine wrapping held tight and only a few lines were visible at the top of pages:

blind drop at night, collapse of the hollow earth theory

And:

Consequences of our actions, no end to incendiary devices

And:

⅔rd hydrogen + AI = the enemy within

Until he had to stop; the words were hurting his head.

The telephone rang. He waited in his hiding place for someone to answer. The muted jangling eventually stopped.

His nerves were too frayed to go on. Face down again, he lowered the strongbox onto the plank; then he backtracked out of the attic, crawling and coughing in the dust, re-enacting the evolutionary process on the way out—hands and knees, coming in a crouch, inflating to full-blown homo erectus. Modern man emerged from the attic blinking in the half-light. The coast was clear, though now that it was gone, he found he missed the scratching sound.

He was halfway across the study when the phone rang again. He paused in front of it, caught in a stare-down with the rotary dial. Answer me! it screeched. Without knowing why—beyond a mounting suspicion that it was his nature to do the wrong thing—he picked up. Burke's voice detonated in his ear.

"Who's this? Who am I talking to?"

"Me," Parker said.

"Well, *me*, get your mother on the line."

"She's not here."

"What? Where the hell is she?"

"Out." Probably with Alf Cooper, he thought. "Where are you?"

Burke explained that he was calling from town, where he'd gone to pick up supplies. "I want to make sure your mother remembers the medicine. She may have a lock on the afterlife, but as far as routines of the day go, her mind's no steel trap."

"Medicine?"

"For Ajax. Old boy's worming again." A pause. "So what're you up to this morning?"

"Uh . . ." He looked blankly at wads of paper on the desk, as if, properly unwrapped, they'd provide an answer. "Getting something to eat."

"Any plans beyond that, or is lounging around the house pretty much the order of the day?"

Instead of responding to the taunt, Parker nudged the bottom drawer open with his foot for another look inside: a Colt single-action revolver with carved eagle and GSP in black enamel in the stock. The sight of the weapon, snuggled in the drawer like some nesting forest creature, emboldened him. "I keep hearing about this book of yours. When do we get to read it?"

"Be forewarned," the old man intoned in his ear. "The book contains ugly secrets about our most revered national heroes.

When it comes to the movers and shakers, I've left no stone unturned."

Which for all Parker knew could be true, except he'd read enough of it himself—*the enemy within, no end to incendiary devices*—to draw his own conclusions.

"Son, where're you taking this call?"

"OK," Parker said hurriedly, "medicine for Ajax, got it—"

"Are you in my study?"

"What? No! Who said anything about—"

"Forced entry, ransacking my personal papers. Is there no end to the list of your abuses?"

"Nobody's ransacking!" Parker said. "I was just curious."

"They tracked you down, didn't they? Pulled your sorry ass out of some cathouse or barrio, brought you in to work on me. Admit it! They'll do anything to keep me from writing the book. They want to know, they *have* to know—am I going to expose the soulless rat bastards or aren't I?"

He decided to let the question dangle. "Here's what *I* think," he said. "I think you did a lot of evil stuff in the old days and now you feel bad about it . . . *maybe*. On the other hand, you got paid a shitload of money to stay quiet about it, and a deal's a deal."

"Exactly," Burke agreed. "My word is my bond."

It was no use. The swagger in his voice always trumped whatever morally superior position Parker had in play, and always pissed him off. "You wrote the damn book anyway! That makes you greedy and a liar *and* a traitor."

Harsh laughter echoed over the phone. "Is that any way to talk to your own flesh and blood?"

"You're not my flesh and—"

The line went dead.

Downstairs a more familiar sound, metal tapping on wood, came from the living room. He found Eugenia stooped over behind the wing chair, her ear pressed to the wall. Tapping it with the cane ever so lightly.

"Just now," Eugenia said. "I was sitting here all by myself when I heard it. Did you?"

"Hear what?"

"Calling for you. Just now."

He took a step back, hands up in front of his face. "That's not funny," he said. His throat was dry. He felt something like the flutter of tiny wings against his rib-cage.

"Your little pet," Eugenia said, tapping the cane on the wall. "Come and listen."

13

Late afternoon: sunlight dwindling on wind-packed snow.

He sat up in bed staring out the window. A crow sailed to earth and landed among trailing arbutus. Across the room the radiator kicked in with a hiss, just as a hand fell on his shoulder. He turned his gaze from the window—and, it seemed, from the brink of coma.

"Time to get dressed."

Walt hovered overhead. He wore a red-checked shirt and lime-green bowtie wedged under the collar. Freshly shaved, his usual bird's nest of thatch-colored hair groomed more or less.

"C'mon! We got a party to go to."

Parker looked at the green bow-tie, uncomprehending. "Party?"

"Better not keep us waiting," Walt said, and disappeared.

Now he remembered: the party at Leo Trunk's farmhouse. The Harvard professor with the walrus mustache who'd taunted him for no reason—*Can it be? The prodigal son here in the flesh?*—as Walt looked on and a snowstorm raged down Main Street. He had no interest in attending such a party, but put on jeans and denim shirt anyway. It was an excuse to get out of the house.

Then Walt and Rita were at the door.

"Ready?" She'd curled thick ringlets in her dark hair, colored her lips bright-red. In high heels and a calico dress, she looked like a gun moll on the run in the Dust Bowl thirties. He was entranced.

"If he ain't ready," Walt said, "he ain't going."

"He's ready. Aren't you ready, Parker?"

"I sure am."

Burke sat in the den polishing the barrels of the twelve-gauge to a bright sheen. Rita kissed his cheek: "We're going, Daddy!" The old man's heavy-lidded gaze fell on Parker, bracing himself for a nasty remark.

"Have fun."

In the kitchen Mother attempted to ply a spoonful of strained peaches between Eugenia's resistant lips. "Open up," she told the old woman. "It's good for you."

Strained peaches—laced with ant-killer? The messy family intrigues felt like a net dropped on him from above, crippling his movements. He pushed past the others, lurched outside to where the night air stabbed his lungs and the cold on his tongue tasted like the purest mineral water. The taste of freedom.

On the road to Rockbridge, and points east.

"Let's get something straight," Walt said, hunched over behind the wheel. "Getting invited to Dr. Trunk's party is a big thing, so nobody's gonna act funny or weird or anything. Understand?"

In his haste to get out of the house, Parker neglected to take a coat; now he sat shivering in the pickup's poorly heated cab. Rita beside him appeared impervious to the weather, even with only a short fur-lined jacket covering her shoulders, a bit ragged around the edges, but still in keeping with G-men and moonshine wars.

"*Understand?*"

Rita nodded.

"Loud and clear," Parker said.

Soon they reached the outskirts of Rockbridge, then the two-block commercial district carpeted in white, snow sculptures of fire hydrants, mail boxes, a '79 Rambler. The Red Hawk Diner looked bereft of customers, all the shops on Main Street and the few houses they passed looking deserted, too, as if the entire population of Rockbridge had skipped town overnight. What do they know that I don't? he wondered.

South of town, the pickup took a long meandering journey he could make no sense of, sharp turns on unpaved roads at alarming speed, never more than ten feet visible in front of them from the truck's weak headlights. Eventually the land flattened out; they drove through miles of snowy countryside. In a far-off field he saw the ghostly silhouettes of cows and horses, grazing.

The pickup came over a ridge and suddenly the moon was there, round and fat and stunningly orange—hanging on the horizon close enough to touch, filling their faces with light in the cab.

"It's the last phase of the lunar cycle," Rita explained. "The moon's at its lowest point right now. If it stays clear like this, it could shine for a week."

Turning, Parker saw twin globes of orange light in her eyes.

The moon guided them for several miles into a forested region. The pickup stopped abruptly at the end of a winding dirt road, and they stepped out under a night sky choked with stars. Clusters of evergreen towering over a dimly lit farmhouse. Close to, in Parker's view, if not exactly in the middle of nowhere.

Cars and trucks parked nearby indicated a good turn-out; but as they hiked through snow to the farmhouse, no sounds could be heard coming from within. Walt stopped on the front porch, confused.

"You think maybe I got the date wrong?"

The weak glow of the porch light exposed rotting floorboards, a trail of gutter slime. He had doubts about entering, but it was too cold to stand around debating it.

"Let's find out," he said, and knocked hard twice.

Party noise erupted inside the clapboard walls—loud music, cocktail laughter, tinkling glasses—as if the guests had been huddled in the dark, waiting to surprise them. The door swung open to Leo Trunk in gray slacks and a yellow après-ski sweater. A blank smile under his walrus mustache.

"Who's this? Who's crashing my party?"

Walt was shocked. "It's us, Doctor Trunk, didn't you say—?"

Trunk spotted Rita; shoving a hand between them, he

drew her in. "Of course! Join the fun!"

In the living room, floor lamps were draped with rainbow-colored scarves, casting a murky light on the festivities. Trunk led them around, making introductions. Bodies flickered in shadow, the air thick with jazz and smoke. He didn't catch any names.

A man with a nose like a pig's snout took Rita's hand and gently kissed it. "Haven't we met somewhere before?" She giggled, but Walt dropped his big hand on his arm, and the pig-man backed away. Trunk took the opportunity to drift off with her, leaving them friendless and alone amid the bubbling revelry.

"What do we do now?" Walt asked.

Parker stared at him, appalled by the clown-tie and utter lack of social graces. He snatched a fresh gin-and-tonic off the coffee table, drank down quickly, and said to Walt: "*Mingle.*" Slipping into the safety of the crowd—more people than he'd expected, in an array of colorful outfits—he wound up in conversation with a red-haired woman and a bearded man in a pinstripe suit. The bearded man gazed at Parker benignly.

"I was just telling Evelyn here about my Experience."

"Yes," Evelyn said breathlessly, in basic black and pearls, "you must hear about Vernon's Experience."

They looked at Parker until he said, "OK."

"On March fifth, 1954," Vernon said, "I found Jesus in the men's room at Grand Central Station."

Somehow Evelyn had worked her way around, hanging now on Parker's arm. "Isn't that *amazing*?" He looked around the living room, thinking: One more drink and I'll be fine.

"March fifth, upper mezzanine, main concourse. Third sink on the left in a row of ten. I'd just finished washing my hands when I looked in the mirror and realized that the face looking back at me wasn't my own. It was the face of Our Lord Jesus Christ." Vernon's tiny eyes shimmered in the half-light. "At that moment, the hoopla and the ruckus, the wild circus called modern life, disappeared from my life. My ears filled with the sound of a heavenly choir. At 4:43 a.m. Eastern Standard Time, He entered my life and I was born again."

Evelyn fondled his chest, whispered in his ear: "You have very intriguing musculature."

"Well?" Vernon asked him. "Have you welcomed Jesus into your life yet?"

Parker shook his head. "Not yet."

"What're you waiting for?"

"Haven't found the right men's room, I guess."

A mini-tsunami of party guests swept him free of Evelyn's grip, deposited him in the kitchen like something washed up on shore. He found a small flotilla of bottles on the counter and poured himself a stiff one, before pressing back into the crowd and letting waves of humanity carry him hither and yon. It ended with him basking in the warmth of a cast-iron wood stove.

"See?" he said, as others swirled by. "One more drink and now I'm fine."

The party seemed to expand and contract, like something passing through the belly of a snake. He met a bank president, a blond anchorwoman, a former linebacker and Heisman trophy-winner who looked forty-five or fifty and wore a threadbare varsity sweater—none of whom, as far as he could tell, with any good reason for being here. What they shared in common were stories about Leo Trunk, his pioneering field work and globe-trotting lifestyle. Trunk, he was told, made first contact with the Yanomano deep inside the Amazon basin. The anchorwoman heard he dined regularly at Buckingham Palace. The bank president recalled Trunk's "stirring" address at an international conference in Sri Lanka, advocating colonies on Mars.

"Leo gets around," he said.

In the kitchen, a tall middle-aged woman in a strapless evening dress extolled the virtues of cosmetic surgery.

"Rhinoplasty," the woman, Sonya, was saying, "a subtle and elegant procedure. The surgeon packs the nose, injects a local, makes incisions along the septal cartilage *here*—" A fingernail sharp as a switchblade nicked the tip of his nose. "—and *here*. Trim it, saw it, chisel, whatever. Quick lateral bone fracture, sew up the nose tips and splint in place. *Voila*! You hardly feel a thing."

Parker, who'd been drinking steadily, gazed at her silver hair and ashen complexion in that fuzzy state where anyone at hand might merit his undying affections. He pictured an athletic seduction, taking this woman of a certain age to the mat like a high-school wrestler. Gradually, it dawned on him; something was wrong.

"Of course," he said politely, "you haven't had it yourself."

Sonya's laugh occupied high decibels. He was further alarmed by five o'clock shadows on her jaw and cheekbone.

"You're too kind," she tittered, "much too kind."

The crowd fetched him up, a slow-moving river of guests, and dropped him next to Walt, who took one look at him and said, "Get lost." His green bow-tie was askew, a bright red palette of shrimp cocktail sauce on his flannel shirt. He returned his attention to Trunk—glass of white wine in one hand, meerschaum pipe in the other—slouched against the counter in a seemingly boneless manner.

"Yeah, OK," Walt said, "what you were saying 'bout high drop-to-lift ratio?"

"In flight," Trunk declared, "two factors are critical—optimum wing angle and most efficient center-of-gravity travel. The latest wind-tunnel research tells us that—"

"Where's Rita?" Parker interrupted.

Trunk looked at him as if for the first time all evening. His ruddy face and alpine-blue eyes suggested a North Seas fisherman, not an Ivy League professor. Swedish? Norwegian? For some reason this ethnic mystery added to his irritation.

"Don't care much for flying myself," he told them. "What's keeping the damn thing up in the air anyway?" With a good-natured slap on the back for Walt: "I mean, where are the strings?"

When outraged like this, Walt's face puffed up like a blowfish. Little gobs of spit hanging off the corners of his mouth. Trunk on the other hand appeared amused.

"I see you have some definite views on the subject."

"Yes," he said, full of drunken pride, "I do."

"Care to tell us about downwash or ground-effect? Maximum rate of climb?"

What he wanted to say was, What's this got to do with paleoanthropology? By now he was convinced the man was a fraud; at the same time he feared for Rita, lost somewhere at this party for transsexuals and born-again Christians. "Has Walt told you about Easter Island?"

"You drunk-ass moron," Walt said. "*He* told me."

"What?"

"A fascinating story," Trunk said. "Did you know that, contrary to popular belief, the indigenous people do not revere the stone heads for which the island is so famous?"

Alcohol, leaps in conversation, the languid tenor sax coming from the living room, induced in him a dream-like state. "I'll be damned," he said.

Walt nodded. "Doctor Trunk knows lots of stuff. He's done just about everything possible."

"And yet, I don't remember a thing."

"Huh?" This remark caught Walt off-guard. "Whaddya mean?"

Sipping the wine, sidestepping a guest in the robes of a Buddhist monk, Trunk described a sunny fall day fifteen years ago when he took a single-engine Piper Cherokee up for a spin above the Pioneer Valley—"Ever seen Quabbin reservoir from the air? Magnificent!"—only to run out of fuel and come plummeting to earth in a two-acre, student-cultivated onion patch on the grounds of Amherst College—". . . ruining an otherwise lovely day."

Rummaging in his pocket, Trunk produced a box of long-stemmed kitchen matches.

"The plane was destroyed, of course, but somehow I walked

off without a scratch . . . or so I thought." Tapping the pipestem on the side of his head. "Tests showed certain injuries had been incurred, damage to neurological centers and so on. As a result, time is a blur to me now. Oh, I can conjure up bits and pieces of a life—my first hair-cut, boot camp at Fort Leonard Wood, dancing naked in the rain on a Yakima Indian reservation. But none of it adds up. Everything's out of whack. I can't say for sure any of it happened to *me*."

Walt was awestruck, but Parker felt sure an elaborate joke was being played out at their expense.

"Needless to say, that was my last flight. I have become, and remain ever since . . . earthbound."

Parker grabbed his brother's arm and shook him from his admiring trance. "Listen to him! Are you listening?"

Walt yanked free. "So what?"

"He's making it up as he goes along!"

"How the hell do you know?"

"Because," he said, but with less conviction, "I do it, too."

Trunk struck a match against the counter and lit his pipe. "More to the point, where's that charming young sister of yours? I want to see how she's getting along."

"But—" Walt was aghast. "What about downwash? Center-of-gravity travel?"

"Enough shop talk. Go find Rita."

Walt scowled, blaming Parker for this.

"Go."

In minutes, the feathery, half-lit crowd swallowed him whole. Closer in, Parker was distracted by the passing parade, men in acrobat tights, a girl wearing stilettos and choke-collar, a big-bellied senior citizen in lederhosen. The Heisman-winner with crew-cut and varsity sweater sat on a folding chair, juggling a half-dozen eggs in the air.

He tore himself away, not without some effort, to look at Trunk. "Can I ask you something?"

"Shoot."

"Are you from Norway or Sweden? Somewhere like that?"

"I," Trunk said, "am a Laplander."

He laughed. "I don't think I ever met a Laplander before."

"Not surprising. We are a reclusive people."

"Arctic Circle, right?"

"Well, in some cases—"

"Icebergs? Eskimos?"

"Yes—"

"Dogsleds! Killer whales!" He couldn't stop himself. "Aurora borealis!"

A chorus of groans as the juggling act came to an end—something in nature abhorring suspended eggs—some cracking on the ex-linebacker's knee, shoulder, top of the head.

"You left out reindeer."

"I was getting to that."

Little pockets of activity flared up in the crowd, guests tripping and shoving, punches drunkenly thrown and missed.

"So what's it like being back home again?"

"I can't describe it," Parker said.

"Try."

He thought as hard as he could. "We're like any other family," he said at last. "We just want to murder each other."

Then things got strange. A man half her size spilled a drink on Sonya's dress. Evelyn sailed by with a firm grip on the bank president's tie. Acrobats pummeled the refrigerator. The pig-faced man squatted in the corner, licking the wallpaper.

Trunk, swept up in the general hysteria, spoke above the din. "All happy families are alike! Each unhappy family is unhappy in its own way!"

A howl of pain from Vernon, who in an apparent test of faith had set the palm of his hand on top of the stove. Now he hopped around the kitchen, scalded red flesh pressed between his legs, yelping like a dog.

"Who among us is beyond reproach?" Trunk shouted. "Who knows the dark urges of their corkscrew heart?"

Parker rubbed his eyes to see better. Was that potted plant on fire? Did a monkey just ride by on a tricycle?

From out of the crowd Rita appeared, her face flushed, dark hair wild and exuberant. "Great party!"

Trunk disengaged himself in a snake-like manner, moving close to her. "They tell me you're a dancer."

"Oh, no," Rita said, blushing. "Nothing like that."

"Have you considered auditioning in Boston? I hear there's a great dance company there."

"No, I couldn't . . ." She looked to Parker, as if for confirmation. "I'm not nearly good enough."

"Who can say? You might be a prima ballerina just waiting to be discovered."

In mounting disbelief, he watched Trunk place a gnarled hand in the small of her back, bend a rude knee between the folds of her calico dress, and sweep Rita up in his arms. "Let me take you away from all this," he said, kissing the underside of her chin.

Someone tugged at Parker's elbow. He looked up into Sonya's tear-stained, androgynous face.

"Help me," she whispered. "I feel so alone . . ."

"You're not the only one." The kitchen light burned his eyes, cool jazz from the living room mutating into a whirlwind of musical genres—punk, ska, heavy metal. He took hold of Rita's arm and freed her from Trunk's embrace; then he stepped forward as if to shake the Laplander's hand, but instead smashed a fist in his face. There was the sharp crunch of septal cartilage, a bystander's mistaken burst of laughter. Trunk slumped to the floor, hands over nose, blood seeping through his fingers. He gazed up at his assailant with the ghost of a smile lurking beneath his walrus mustache.

"I guess what they say is true."

"What?" Parker demanded. "What's true?"

"You can't go home again."

He might have struck him again, but the crowd, sensing new violence in its midst, shifted amoeba-like to find him. He bobbed and weaved, pushing through a tangle of arms and legs and out the back door, into a sudden hush of wind and stars. The cold spurred him downhill toward a dark structure set off by evergreens: a barn, with flimsy ramshackle doors that fell open to his touch and a stench of rusted implements and pigeon shit. Some light pierced the slatted roof; as objects took shape he saw abandoned pig pens, empty feed troughs, and parked face-first and towering overhead—a silver-striped single-engine Wendt *Traveler.*

Moonlight glittered along the fuselage, off the propellers

and varnished landing gear. The plane's wingspan engulfed the barn's interior; it crouched in the dark like some great cat predator.

Footsteps were coming, but he didn't hear them until they were right behind them. "Check this out," he said to whichever of Trunk's morally depraved guests had followed him down here, when the back of his head erupted in pain and he found himself dropping backward in baffling free-fall, ending only when he hit the ground. Somewhere overhead, Walt was shouting.

"I *can* fly! I can!"

Parker closed his eyes and drifted with the pain, earthbound.

3

THE FROZEN LAKE

14

Trees whirled past the window. Snow-covered hills seemed to roll into the sky. Rita fought back tears as the pickup barreled home.

"I can't stand it any more! What are you all protecting me from?"

"Me?" Walt tried to drive and protest his innocence at once. "What did I do?"

Parker's ear throbbed violently each time the truck hit a pothole.

"Tell me! I want to know what's going on!"

"Just a little longer," Walt pleaded. "It'll be different after that."

"After *what*? After we fly to Easter Island?"

"It's true," Parker said, or meant to; his tongue flopped uselessly in his mouth and he settled for dangling his injured head out the window, jowls rippling in the night breeze, a dog's life.

For awhile in bed he floated, eyes open, arms spread wide, bathed in a spectral light like stars glowing on the deck of an ocean liner. A pervasive numbness gathered in his legs, paralysis in body and soul. Not sleeping or awake or dead, just . . . floating.

A sudden crash shook the room: windows rattled, the floor trembled. He sat up, looked around. First there was middle-of-the-night silence and then—again!—the sound a child's body might make being thrown against a wall. Still dressed in last night's clothes, he went to the hall for a better look. Empty, every door closed as it should be. A dream? He was nearly convinced of it when the door to Burke's study opened.

He slid back in his room. Burke's study: tiny scribbled notes, hidden strongbox, ivory-handled Colt in the bottom desk drawer. He'd stood at that desk eyeing the gun while on the phone with—Burke!

Footsteps trudged by. He peeked out in time to see a hulking figure in long johns—broad-beamed shoulders, tousled hair—headed downstairs. A moment later he followed, making his way in the dark with newly recovered navigational skills. This might be a dream after all; it had that quality.

The front hallway was damp, more like fog than darkness. Parker stepped in something warm and sticky. Kneeling, he sought the warm spot with his hand. There it was, and another, a trail leading to the kitchen. Dark odorless film covered his fingers. Without knowing why, he tasted it; the warm stuff was bitter on his tongue.

Not spaghetti sauce. Not this time.

Walt faced the kitchen window, his underwear caught in

the moon's halo effect. A glint of light came off his right side, and Parker looked hard to see what he held there—a *blade,* he thought, and froze against the wall. Axe blade, axe murder.

And just like that the awful crime flashed in his imagination: Walt sneaking into the study, coming up behind the old man, raising the axe and bringing it down. Staggering downstairs in his long johns, bloodlust ringing in his ears. *Just a little longer. It'll be different after that.*

He glanced around the corner to make sure; this time Walt was looking back. "Who's there?" But Walt couldn't see him because he wasn't wearing his glasses. Somehow this was the most disturbing detail of all.

Before anything else, he should run upstairs and look for himself. But the thought of what he might find was vastly unreal to him; even seeing a hacked-up torso and limbs with his own eyes might not persuade him. The kitchen door opened and shut. At the window he saw Walt marching through snow, apparently barefoot, headed for the stone wall. One hand clutched the axe, in the other something vaguely round, dark and clotted, like a basketball with hair.

As it turned out, seeing *was* believing. What little he'd had to eat all day rose in his stomach; pushing open the door he leaned over the porch railing and threw up in the rhododendron. To his surprise, the frost-lined shrubbery began to shake violently.

"Hey!" a voice cried out. "Stop that!"

Parker retreated, coughing, spitting, wiping his mouth. "What? Who?"

"Shhhh," the voice said. "It's me."

A short, hooded figure emerged, crossed to the bottom steps of the porch. Where the figure's military-style raincoat fell open, he saw a tin badge affixed to an olive-drab shirt. Police! How could they get here so fast?

"Where is he?" Alf Cooper asked.

"Who?"

"Who? Who else? Look, just tell me. Is the old man upstairs sleeping or out lurking around like you?"

For once, it was clear what to do: alert the authorities—one of whom happened to be conveniently placed right in front of him—and make sure the rest of the family was OK. Instead he hoped Alf hadn't seen Walt or noticed the bloody footprints in the snow behind him.

"Both," he finally answered. "Sort of."

"Well then . . ." Alf started across the threshold, but found his way blocked.

"Wait a minute—don't you need a warrant or something?"

"Warrant for what?"

The two men looked at each other, puzzled.

"Just so you understand," Alf said. "I'm doing this as a favor for your mother. She wanted some thug off the street to do it, but I told her you're much better off going with my many years in law enforcement." He hitched up the belt on his pants. "After all this time, you could say I'm an expert on thinking like a bad guy."

"I don't," Parker said.

"Don't what?"

"Understand."

A howl came from the woods, sharp and loud and over

in a second. Alf spun on his heel, a hand dropping to the gun in his holster, certain to discover what Parker didn't want discovered. A jagged line of icicles hung off the underside of the gutter. He reached up, snapped off the biggest one and lunged at Alf—"*En garde!*"—playfully skewering the lawman in his ample midsection. Alf didn't get the joke; he toppled backward with a woman's startled cry and landed in the shrubs. When he regained his footing, he regarded Parker with a look of great sadness and disappointment.

"What the hell did you do that for?"

"Sorry."

He dropped the icy weapon. The night air, reverting to silence, seemed to calm them both.

"She offered to pay me," Alf said, "but I couldn't take her money. I seen what the son of a bitch's done to her over the years. I seen how it'd be no great loss if he was to just . . . *turn up* somewhere." He shrugged. "It was your mother's idea. Said you wouldn't mind."

Parker looked up at the moon, had no problem picturing it looking back down and laughing at him. He laughed, too, out of sheer fright.

"What's so goddamn funny?"

"Nothing." He stopped laughing, since basically it wasn't funny—while what was left of the family slept upstairs, Walt roamed the woods with a severed head and he stood on the porch discussing murder-for-hire with the deputy sheriff. There were other, more pressing things to attend to, but one question delayed him. "What were you planning, exactly?"

"Planning?"

"Yeah. While you were hiding in the bushes."

"Not sure." Alf scratched the back of his neck. "Figured it'd come to me when I got here."

"Go home."

"Huh?"

"You can't help here."

"But your mother—"

"I know, I know. It was her idea." Gently Parker steered him around the side of the house toward where he'd parked on the side of the road. First off, he thought, if you want to be a hit-man, leave the patrol car at home. Alf paused in the snow under the rock elm to share his own thoughts.

"A damn shame, you know? A man's home is his castle, 'cept when it's not, things go bad and you've got to get out or let the others leaves. Know what I mean? One thing leads to another, somebody gets in the way, and the whole family suffers, like the torture of the damned. *You* —!" he cried, pointing a finger. "You're the smart one, you tell me! Where's a man at if he don't got his family?"

"Up a creek," Parker replied. "No hope of a paddle."

"Damn right."

"By the way, about you and my mother . . ."

"Yeah?"

"It's OK by me."

Alf smiled, his pudgy face relaxing as a single muscle. "Thanks, Parker." He plodded the rest of the way to the road where he sat in the patrol car for several long minutes. Finally the engine started up and the patrol car rolled into the night.

Grabbing a coat and boots, Parker struck off for the trees.

In the deep woods, cold dug beneath his protective clothing and invaded his bones. Past the hole Walt left in the barbed wire perimeter, past the first row of trees, stars dimmed out overhead, what light there was giving way to blanket darkness.

A twig cracked. He ducked behind a tree, peering into a moonlit frost hollow a short distance away. Walt kicked at a tree stump until it fell over in a bed of dead leaves and larch cones, then sat in his bloodstained underwear and stared at the ground—axe hanging from one hand, the hateful object he'd been carrying in the other dropped in nearby shadows. Are the eyes open? Parker wondered. Is it smiling?

Some time passed. A dog barked in the distance, followed by the high-pitched squeal of a horseshoe hare.

How should he announce himself without provoking a violent attack? No good answer presented itself, so he decided to step into a ragged patch of moonlight and take his chances. Walt perked up, sniffing the air, squinting in his general direction. Otherwise he didn't seem to care all that much.

"Nice night," he said. "Clear, not too windy. Good night for flying."

Just as clear, Parker's vision of the immediate future: Walt arrested and tried for murder, a speedy conviction, life behind bars. In this vision Eugenia and Mother aged and died quickly, leaving only Rita to care for.

"Is this what you had in mind all along?" he asked.

Walt shrugged. "Somebody had to."

"I thought we were going to talk about this first."

"Talk about what? I took a few swipes and that was that. No

big deal." Stifling a yawn. "Left a mess in the study, though."

"That's what I mean. A mess."

"Huh?"

He gestured to where his stepfather's decapitated remains lay just out of sight in the snow. "You hack him up into little pieces and you're *bored?*"

"This?" Walt retrieved his trophy, rose to his full height and advanced on him, a grinning lunatic in long johns, brandishing a scalp that smelled both foul and sickly-sweet. "Is this what you're talking about?"

He couldn't help it, he had to look. But the eyes staring back at him were feral and black, the row of teeth shiny as razors, a flat pug nose bunched up in a snout. It wasn't Burke's head. It wasn't a head at all.

"The window was open. It flew in the study. Didn't you hear it banging into the walls?"

Up close, the bloated mass of hair and tissue took on definition: stiff claws, double-winged membranes, dead eyes that seemed to see inside his soul.

"Bat!" he said. "That's a bat."

"What the hell else?" Walt shook his head. "My own brother—I got to wonder what it is you're accusing me of."

"Hard to say," he said, frightened and relieved.

With another ferocious howl, Walt swung around like a discus-thrower and hurled the dead bat into the air. It landed somewhere in the dark with a dull flat sound. Then he seized Parker by the coat and jammed him against a tree.

"I'm telling you for the last time! Stay out of it!" An elbow in Parker's throat precluded a response; the more he struggled, the harder he was pinned to the tree. "I had to go back in there, had to say goodnight to Doctor Trunk with him bleeding all over the place, people looking at me like *I'm* the one popped him in the nose, 'Uh, thanks for the party, Doctor Trunk, sorry 'bout what happened to your face . . .'"

"I didn't," Parker gasped from under the chokehold. "—didn't—like—"

"What? Didn't like what?"

"—how he—treated—Rita—"

"Yeah," Walt had to admit it. "I saw that, too." With that his murderous impulse vanished, he let go, seemed to retreat into himself. Parker gasped for air, rubbing his neck until airways were properly restored.

"What the hell is it anyway? I see guys in town hit on her all the time but I never thought Doctor Trunk would." A sheepish smile came over his face. "Sorry I hit you so hard."

Parker touched the welt behind his ear. "Forget it."

"Really? You mean it? You forgive me?"

"Sure. We're brothers. That's what brothers do."

The good feeling between them threatened to form into a permanent bond; but the half-crazed, would-be axe-murderer was too skittish for that, already brooding on other things.

"This don't change nothing, what Doctor Trunk did. We're still getting out of here."

"In his plane."

"Ain't his anymore. He gave it to me, said if I fixed it up, it's mine." To Parker's skeptical look: "He *did*. Hey, you think it's easy rebuilding a airplane engine from scratch? How many people you know ever did that? How many with *brain damage*?"

He had to agree: "It's amazing." Walt meanwhile paced back and forth, still clutching the axe. "So what happens when you get there?"

"I got it figured out. We'll build a hut on Anakei Bay, raise some goats and pigs. Visit *Los Siete Monos*. Rita wants to see the wild horses."

"Rita's not going anywhere. Not while the old man's around."

"The old man—*shit*." Walt draped his face in his hands and started to cry—softly, in contrast to his killer howls. "I tried, you know? When we were growing up I tried everything I could think of to make him happy—not proud or anything, just so maybe he'd *like* me a little." Tears seeped through his blood-caked fingers. "Now all I can think of is, what's the best way to make him die?"

"There's lots of ways," Parker said thoughtfully. "Thing is, it has to look like an accident."

Walt squinted, until comprehension dawned. "Yeah, OK. I get it. We pour kerosene down his throat."

"Won't look like much of an accident."

"Drown him in the tub. Lock him in the garage with the motor running. Bury him alive."

What *is* the best way? he thought. The revelation of the bat's demise left certain expectations dangling; if he was being honest with himself, the horror he'd felt at the old man's beheading was more like gratitude that someone had done his dirty work for him.

"What the hell, you wanna come along?" Walt asked. "I can fix the seats for three. Then you get to see the wild horses, too!"

In fact, lunching on pineapple and papaya juice in the shade of a thirty-ton stone face overlooking the South Pacific seemed right now like the best of all possible worlds. Parker threw an arm around his shoulders and squeezed.

"You talked me into it."

15

"How was the party?"

Late morning, in the kitchen again. Mother sat at the breakfast table in floppy slippers and a blue chamois robe. Her face was puffy, hair frazzled as after electroshock therapy. Parker, having slept little himself, joined her for a breakfast of runny eggs and lukewarm coffee. If she looks that bad, he thought, what about me? His ear ached where Walt struck him. His head felt like a sealed tomb.

"*Well?*" Mother asked.

"Fun," he said. "It was . . . fun."

"I thought I heard noises last night. But when I got up to look, nothing was there."

"What kind of noises?"

"Thumping and banging, all kinds of commotion."

He knew what she'd heard. "A dream," he told her.

"Yes," Mother agreed, "that must be it. Noises in my dreams."

Or the sounds of bat-murder—Walt's flailing attack on the winged mammal invading their premises—and later, Parker on his hands and knees scrubbing away gobs of fur and blood, as well as far too much slimy pink viscera. Walt cowered in the corner, useless to help with clean-up. Parker guided him to his bedroom, slinking off into his own, where he stood at the window fighting the urge to bay at the moon.

When he woke from this reverie, Mother was gazing at him—as if he might be the answer to her dreams, but kept coming up short.

"What?"

"Nothing," she said.

The back door flew in and Ajax strolled in; one look at leftovers and he sprang ahead, front paws planted on the table, and lapped at bacon-and-egg residue with a puppyish *joie de vivre*. "No! Stay away!" she shouted. Parker elbowed the old dog away, Ajax snarling back in a toothless show of menace.

Now Burke loomed up in brush pants and hunting vest, ever-present Remington twelve-gauge by his side. "Am I interrupting?"

"No more than usual," Parker said.

He entered anyway, tracking slush and snow on the linoleum. Parker, about to protest on Mother's behalf, saw what dangled from each gloved fist—mallards, a pair of them, with matching collars and luminous blue-green feathers.

"Jump-shot these beauties down at the lake—last of 'em, too. Won't see any more till spring. From here on, ice-fishing's the only game in town. Done much ice-fishing lately, son?"

"It's on my to-do list," he said.

Burke dropped the ducks in the sink, began yanking off clumps of feathers in his big hands. In the lingering gloom of his hangover, Parker imagined they weren't just the last ducks of the season but possibly the last remaining mallards on earth. Somehow the old man had rendered extinct an entire species, all by himself and all before breakfast. For that alone, Parker thought, he should pay.

"I wish he wouldn't do that in the sink," Mother said. "I've asked a million times."

"Well," Burke said, with his back to her, "maybe not a *million*." Now he displayed a sheath knife in one hand and a mallard's skillfully plucked neck in the other. "Son, there's an art to preparing wildfowl."

"No," he said. "Uh-uh. Not interested."

"Of course you are. Observe."

A hissing sound broke the previous silence, as the knife sliced through rubbery sinew. Blood drained into a pan in the sink, releasing a sharp tang of feathers and wet entrails into the air. He noticed Mother beside him staring at the ritual in a fascinated trance.

"We chill the blood while the duck's being cooked," Burke explained. "It's used as thickener, strained and added to the sauce at the very last minute. Oh, and don't forget, add one and a half tablespoons of vinegar to prevent clotting."

Mother snapped out of her trance. "I never said I'm cooking that."

"And the sauce must be kept at a constant simmer. Once blood's been introduced, don't ever let it come to a boil."

"Did you hear what I said? I'm *not going to*—"

Turning, Burke raised the knife to a spot just under his chin and mimicked drawing the blade across his own leathery throat—a pantomime of sufficient authenticity to shock her into silence.

"I told you, no more of this shit," Parker said. "It has to stop."

In his boots and camouflage vest, Burke resembled a jungle fighter, aged now, sent out to pasture. He set the knife on the counter. "I'd best heed your words or risk inciting another senseless act of violence." To Mother: "Did you hear about the fracas at last night's party? Your son here got stupidly drunk and assaulted a college professor—Harvard, no less! We'll be lucky if they don't toss us all in the hoosegow."

Mother looked from son to husband and back again. "What's he talking about?"

"I . . . It's a long story."

The old man snickered.

"You bastard," Parker said. "*You* ought to be locked up."

"Well, what about you?"

"What's that got to—"

"What are you but the worst kind of hopped-up, good-for-nothing parasite of the system? And compulsive liar to boot." His poisonous indignation fouled the air. "*Condominios en los Tropicos,* my ass! I spent a lifetime in the trade. Don't you think I know a shitload of disinformation when I hear it?"

For Mother, it was the last straw; she tucked her head inside her folded arms and started to cry. A moment passed. He stood and approached Burke at the counter, any number of things going through his head.

"Who told you that?"

Up close, his stepfather smelled of soil and gunpowder. "I have my sources."

"I don't care what you say about me." He kept his voice low, so as not to disturb Mother. "Just leave her out of it."

Burke pinched a stray mallard feather off his sleeve, held it up for closer study. "Son, it's been three days now since you first graced us with your presence. I consented, if only for the sake of your poor mother. She drinks, you know." A gentle puff, the feather sailed aloft, came to rest beside the sheath knife on the counter. "But I think we can all agree, your conduct overall has been less than perfect. Has been, in fact, shocking and reprehensible."

There was gentle snoring behind them; Mother had cried herself to sleep. Briefly he felt robbed of all initiative. "Can I say something here?"

"Fire away."

"First off—you're a cold-hearted son of a bitch who doesn't deserve the family he's got. And don't take this wrong, but I'm pretty sure you're out of your mind. My feeling is, it's time for you to go."

Burke laughed. "That's what *I* was going to say."

"What?"

"Let's be clear on one thing, son. Whatever you may think, you're here in this house strictly as a guest. Unlike your mother, I'm free of any misguided sentiment toward you. Have been since a long time ago."

In every respect he felt himself the better man here, but the words stabbed at his heart. "Me too."

"That's it? No remorse? No inner turmoil over staying away all these years? Come on, son, you can tell me. Haven't I always been like a father to you?"

He groped for the knife but angry red spots dancing before his eyes obscured its location. Burke claimed it first, and the brief struggle was ended.

"All this by way of saying—time's come for another of your pointless journeys of discovery. Take another five years. Take all the time you like. Understand? This is *not your home.*"

At the table, Mother snored. Parker felt giddy at the speed with which pretenses were dropping around him. A deranged smile crept to his lips. "I was going to warn you," he said menacingly. "That's really all I had in mind."

A gratifying flicker of uncertainty crossed the old man's face. "Fine. We're in agreement. Tonight we have a festive meal together. Tomorrow you leave."

He resumed plucking feathers, humming while he worked. Mother was slumped over the breakfast table; if she stayed in the chair much longer, her joints would ache all day. He helped her to her shaky feet as Burke broke into song, delivered with revival-tent zeal:

A-ma-zing grace, how sweet the sound
That saved a wretch like meeee . . .

In late afternoon he decided on a walk. Ajax barked once, declaring his interest, and tagged along.

The sun was bright in the cloudless sky, the air brisk and

cold. Ajax hopped in and out of snowdrifts bordering the road, even chased a willow branch idly tossed his way. Then he caught sight of something and loped over the hill.

Heading into a stand of white pine, he no longer felt oppressed by the cold; now the winter's presence was like an old friend, an ally, a source of strength. Any fool can see what has to be done, he thought. Besides, there was the strongbox to consider.

He came to a clearing, saw a red-tailed hawk circling low in the sky. Suddenly it went into a dive, vanishing in scrub brush before shooting skyward again, fresh kill—mole, vole, ground squirrel—trapped in its talons.

A twig cracked nearby. He didn't see anything at first, only because he failed to prepare for what actually stood less than fifteen feet away—a bull moose, six feet at the shoulder, a good thousand pounds or more, standing in a patch of dead sawgrass. *Burke's* moose, the legendary one he'd been hunting for years, the air around it thick with its musky scent. Now the legend held powers of life and death over him—sudden, hoof-grinding death—Parker could see it shine in the beast's flat eyes. The moose rotated shovel-shaped antlers toward him, spewing great clouds of steam from its nostrils. One step and I'm dead, he thought. He didn't move, didn't breathe, only waited for what would happen next.

Nothing happened. The moose shook its antlers and trotted off through fetlock-deep snow into the woods.

Memories gather, he realized, they accumulate, more and more until the weight they take on is crushing. Life in the house years ago was bad enough; now getting through each day was a struggle, immersed yet again in the family and all it ever meant to him, somehow always more than the sum of its parts. Moose, winter, family, death.

I know I can count on you, Mother said, *for whatever needs doing.*

The last light of day melted into living room furniture as it had done since his childhood, possibly since the dawn of man, an eternal blemish on side-chairs and flame-stitched sofa.

Eugenia sat in the wing chair, staring into the fireplace. "Times are tough," she said, as he entered. "I know. I've seen it before."

"No doubt," he said.

Slowly and with great effort, she turned toward him. Embers glowed off her trifocals.

"This house," she said. "It's like a great big living thing. It talks to me. It says, in good times everyone's happy, not a care in the world. But when times get tough, you better watch out. Better hold on for all your worth so's not to get sucked in." Innumerable wrinkles pinched the corners of her mouth. "Times are tough. I know, I've seen it before. People cannot be trusted."

Parker looked at daguerreotypes on the mantel, rows of cruel, accusing sepia-toned faces. "Eugenia, I couldn't agree more."

"Just tell me one thing," she said.

"What's that?"

"Is the Ice King coming soon?"

"Yes," he assured her. "Real soon."

Faint light drew him to Rita's open bedroom door. Inside, a tapered candle burning on the dressing table caused shadows to dance along the wall and the empty bed, across the front of the paperback biography of Balanchine on the night-stand. Rita stood at the window, her hair like a splash of water down the back of her lavender spaghetti-strap tights.

As he came in she looked over at him, her beautiful face shockingly inert; he might as well have been a total stranger.

"Where's everyone at?" he asked.

"Walt took Mother to town for groceries. Daddy's out hunting, I guess."

"Can't be. He already shot the last ducks on earth."

"What?"

"Forget it."

He joined her by the window as the sun dropped below treetops. The bedroom succumbed, by inches, to a hazy granular light. "When we were kids we used to play down at the lake all the time. It got cool at night and you could hear thousands of bullfrogs croaking in the dark."

Rita shrugged. "It could've happened, even if I don't remember. That's what Leo says."

"Who?"

"Doctor Trunk. He says there's things he can't remember, but that doesn't mean they didn't happen."

He shook his head clear of the awful name. "I remember what it's like living out here. Like nothing ever changes. This is how it was, this is how it is now, this is how it's going to be forever."

"Things changed after you came back." Candlelight showed the distress on her face. "I know we're acting crazy, but you have to believe me, it was different before. We finally had some peace in the house. Mother and Daddy weren't fighting, Walt was busy fixing cars, and I—"

"You had a boyfriend."

Rita flinched, as though he'd struck her. "What?"

"Some kid from up by Great Barrington wanted to marry you—"

"No, that didn't—"

"Get you out of here—"

"It wasn't like that," she said, starting to tremble.

"He was right," Parker said. "You have to get out."

"What about the others?"

"Leave. Right now. With me."

She slumped against the wall, giving way to tears. He took hold of her shoulders to calm her. This torment was unforgivable, but circumstances demanded it. In the end she'd be grateful for grass huts and palm trees, a place where brother and sister could live, far beyond the pale of smaller minds.

"I see things," she said. "Last night, after the party. I saw people sitting in the snow, in a circle. There was a sound like shattering glass. Someone had a gun."

His own dream of ghost-girls swirling on ice came back to him. Gun? It wasn't how *he* saw it.

A breeze rustled the curtains. He came close and kissed her. Her tongue flicked in his mouth, a low moan building in her throat as his hand trailed over her breast and ribs and a belly that wasn't there, coming to rest on the soft cloth-covered mound between her legs—the brute pleasure of going too far, rapid death's-edge flutter of the heart. Finally they let go. She stepped back, all confusion gone from her sea-green eyes, shaded now with their own dark urgency.

Shadows claimed one side of her body from candlelight. One side of her face was visible, one shoulder and hip, one dancer's foot curled on the floor. Her hand reaching out in darkness tugged the shoulder-strap down, exposing one small pale breast, one acorn-brown nipple.

"This, too," she said. "I saw this, too."

16

"Dinner!"

The call from downstairs froze them both—somehow they'd come to believe the house was empty—and now they came apart, like boxers returning to separate corners. Rita pulled the strap up on her shoulder, had nothing to say.

"Dinner's ready!"

For Parker, the voice from below echoed to an eight-year-old boy playing in the woods on an autumn afternoon. Hearing the distant cry, the boy wipes out a twigs-and-dirt Army fort with the back of his hand, runs out of the woods across the backyard to a home-cooked meal in a big warm house.

Not a bad life, he thought. Not bad and not mine.

"Last time I'm calling!"

Staring at him in the half-light, Rita called back: "Coming!"

His first night home, he'd been impressed by the dining room's well-preserved ambience—the sparkling cutlery, fresh lilies inside a teardrop vase. Tonight he saw paint chipping off the china cabinet and a hairline crack running through the French door.

Burke sat at the head of the table in a white shirt and tweed jacket. "Ummm, smell that wildfowl . . . Hello?" he said. "Ship to shore? Anyone read me?"

Hours earlier, driven to the point of madness, he'd groped wildly for the sheath knife with which to skewer his stepfather. His rage had cooled since then, become something pure and focused, complete in itself. "Yeah, I read you."

"Good." Burke slapped the chair to his right. "Have a seat."

From the kitchen, Rita called out: "What about Eugenia?"

This authentic bit of family lore—fetching Eugenia for dinner—cheered him slightly. In years past he'd found her wandering the attic, seated beneath the rock elm or perched uncertainly on the pickup's rear bumper, gazing at the stars. This time he found her in the living room, struggling to rise from the wing chair. Loudly she spurned his offer to help.

"Get back!" The steel tip of the walking cane poked inches from his face. "I can do it."

So he hung back, watching the old woman's shaky progress down the hall, cheered further by her tough Yankee spirit.

"Food on the table?" she barked. "How come I'm always last to know?"

In spite of domestic tensions choking the air, the dinner awaiting them was up to Mother's high standards—a dizzying array of salad and cooked vegetables, more than he could take in all at once, set on the table in a rich, wood-smoked panoply, all anchored by the roast duck, cooked to a delicate brown, on a serving tray in the center of the table.

As he placed Eugenia in the chair next to his, Rita came in from the kitchen with a plate of braised celery. She wore a cotton sweater and denims threadbare at the knee. Her hair was pulled back severely. She sat across the table, avoiding any notice of him. Walt beside her stared into his soup bowl, exuding gloom.

Mother was still fussing in the kitchen; Burke leaned over the table and inclined his head to shout through the doorway. "Let's get cracking, shall we?" She hurried in, pale and perspiring, and sat at the opposite end. Folding hands, she led the family in prayer.

"Lord, for what we're about to receive, we thank you."

All heads bowed—an opportunity to take a look around, at Walt with his eyes squeezed shut in fierce concentration, Burke appearing to doze off, Eugenia with one eye open winking at the wall.

"—through Your grace, a family again . . ."

And Rita, whose eyes stayed down no matter how hard he urged her not to, in his head. *A moose*! he shouted silently. *There was a moose!*

"—keep us safe from harm . . ."

Could've gored me, trampled me, torn me to shreds.

"—and blessed in the bounty of Your everlasting love . . ."

But it didn't. It was a sign.

"Amen."

The clanging plates and bowls moved Ajax to bark from the corner. Over the commotion, Burke addressed Mother directly. "Did you remember to rinse the insides with brandy?"

"Yep," she said, reaching for the wine bottle.

"Greased 'em with ginger and lemon?"

"Yes *sir*."

Apparently satisfied, Burke commenced slicing and loading generous portions of duck onto plates offered up by Rita. Eugenia sat before a plate of steamed asparagus and three-bean salad, looking stumped.

"Is that it?" she asked Mother. "What about soup?"

"No soup."

"Any chowder?"

"No," Mother said, less patiently. "Since when do you want chowder?"

The old woman nudged Parker's rib. "It's that funny taste. I do like that."

Each family member's style of consumption was unique. Walt gulped food down as if it might be snatched away at any time. Burke used knife and fork to carve tidy, self-contained cubes of duck meat. Rita barely touched her meal, Mother seemed intent on the wine. Parker was just plain hungry; he finished his serving of duck, yams, asparagus and salad, and promptly asked for more.

"For someone who claims to abhor blood sports," Burke noted, "you sure can put it away."

He paused, mid-bite, to answer. "It's the blood in the sauce. I do like that."

Across the table Walt was glaring at him; whatever rough-and-tumble camaraderie had sprung up between them the night before was gone. When it seemed he could no longer stand it, he blurted out: "Where you been all day?"

Parker avoided glancing at Rita. "Around."

"'Around'? What's that mean?"

"In the area. The general vicinity."

"Yeah? Well, I didn't ever see you in the general vicinity—"

Burke interrupted, raising his glass: "A toast." The others joined him. Toast to what? Parker wondered. God and country? Pissing in the *Führerbunker?*

"To Parker," his stepfather said. "It's been good as hell having him back among us."

One by one, the others looked at him. Waiting.

"Well," he said, "it's been uh good to be here."

Something brushed his knee. Under the table he saw a grizzled snout rooting around in Eugenia's lap, particularly since she was scraping celery bits and chopped-up asparagus into Ajax's gaping jaw, and giggling while she did so.

"Stop that," he whispered.

"Oh hush. The poor thing hasn't eaten in weeks."

Burke meanwhile gave an after-dinner dab of the napkin to his lips and announced: "Son, a call came for you today. Long-distance. You weren't around so I took a message."

Parker looked at him. Long-distance?

"Bad news, I'm afraid. You're needed on the coast."

This made no sense for an embarrassingly long time, until he recalled dinner the other night, his elaborate accounts of high-stakes Mexican real-estate deals, a suite of offices in Beverly Hills, Olympic-sized pools in Malibu. *Condominios en los Tropicos.*

"Details are sketchy, but definite trouble brewing at corporate HQ. Graft, corruption, blood in the boardroom, a whole lot of shit—excuse my French, ladies—hitting the fan." Burke sipped his wine. "They called, son. You're needed on the coast."

Parker laughed, expecting the others to join in; looking around the table, he was disappointed to find that no one did. Mother and Rita looked shaken by the news. Walt stared, open-mouthed.

He looked back at his stepfather. "I think you should have let me take that call."

"Does that mean I get his room?" Eugenia melded her fossilized hands in the approximate shape of a shoebox. "Mine's not nearly big enough for me *and* the airplane."

Burke smiled. "What airplane is that, Mother?"

"Ask Walt," the old woman said, leering at them. "He can tell you."

"What? Huh? I don't know what she's talking about . . . " But under the family's withering scrutiny, it didn't take Walt long to crack. "Ain't no big deal," he grumbled. "I've been working on the engine for more'n six months."

Burke nodded, as if being told secrets of incalculable value. "And where are you headed, if I may ask? Somewhere in particular or off into the wild blue yonder?"

Across the table, Parker watched his brother fight to control himself, and lose. "Yeah, goddamn it, somewhere in particular! We're gonna fly to—"

"No," Rita said sharply. All heads turned to her. "We're not flying anywhere. There isn't any plane."

Walt gasped at this betrayal. "Yeah there is!"

No one but Parker believed him, and he might have said so had he not been distracted by furtive motion on his right—

Eugenia bent over sideways, sliding a large quantity of yams down Ajax's throat. Parker seized the plate, kicked the old dog away. Things were happening too fast; he needed time to think.

"Wild blue yonder," Eugenia said dreamily. "The last time I was up in the clouds was 1909, when my dear departed Calvin took me for a ride in a hot-air balloon. A storm caught us over Marblehead and carried us out to sea." She sighed. "It was the most profoundly romantic moment of my life."

Burke poured more wine all around. "In any event, I'm sure we all agree, it's been great having Parker among us, if only for a few days."

During this interlude, everyone had a chance to collect themselves with varying degrees of success. Rita hung back, looking wary. Walt's face was a mask of confusion. Mother sat in casual silence, her grip on the wine-glass firm and unyielding.

"And now we learn Walt's leaving us as well," the old man said. "Bit by the bug, eh? Want to see the big city? Walk a few mean streets?"

"... Yeah."

"Completely natural, of course, the young leaving the nest and all. It's in the nature of things. The future looms before you like an infinitely bright horizon."

"The world is your oyster," Eugenia added.

"Shut up!" Mother yelled. "Shut up! Shut up! Shut up!"

Rita touched her wrist. "Mother ..."

"Well, I don't understand what's happening, and *she's* no help at all." But her daughter's touch soothed her nerves; after a long sip of wine, she addressed the table in general. "Sorry. Didn't mean to shout."

By now Parker had had a chance to regroup, determined to go on the offensive for a change. "The nature of things, is that what we're talking about? Then you can understand why I'm taking Rita with me." Surprise rippled over the faces of his loved ones. "I was thinking about it anyway, before you took that . . . call. It's the right thing to do."

She looked at him as if they'd never spoken before, let alone nearly made love. *Hello?* he thought irritably. *Ship to shore? Do you read me?*

Walt's fist slammed on the table-top. "Pass the gravy."

"I was talking—"

"Just pass the goddamn gravy."

To everyone's further surprise, Mother agreed with Burke. "It's true, I had this silly notion you'd stay for awhile, but now I realize that was wrong. You have a life of your own to live and you should be out there living it." Flashing a venomous glance at her mother-in-law: "Where's it written that children have to stay home and watch the old folks wither and die?"

"No one's leaving," Rita said.

"Well, dear, sooner or later we—"

"No! We're all home again, like a real family. Look how long that's taken. We're not giving up now, are we?" She turned to Walt. "*Are we?*"

"Uh-uh," Walt said.

"What about his room?" Eugenia demanded. "We haven't decided that—" She stopped, letting out a soft, choked cry. A series of convulsions shook her tiny frame, like prairie winds rustling through a scarecrow's ragged clothes. Her eyes rolled in her head, a knobby tongue poking from her toothless gums.

Just as quickly, it was over. Eugenia took a deep breath, folded her napkin and carefully laid it on the table.

"He's here," she said in the direction of the chandelier. "I didn't expect him so soon, but you never can tell."

Slowly she rose to her feet, a doddering scarecrow in widow's weeds, and with the aid of the cane left the dining room the same way she came in, under her own steam. A moment passed. Parker looked around at his bewildered clan.

"The Ice King," he explained. "Seems he's come back early."

A short time later in the den, he stood by the pool table nursing a brandy as the old man settled in the armchair with a snifter of his own.

"That's some story you told us. 'Trouble at HQ, son. They need you on the coast.' Very clever."

Burke rubbed his face wearily. "I was offering you a graceful way to bow out. Can't we at least hope for that?"

Evidently a rhetorical question, since he closed his eyes and went to sleep. Parker knelt beside him for a closer look. Sleep made mush of his stepfather's iron jaw, the lines in his face smooth as baby fat. In a distant childhood he no longer recognized as his own, Parker had worshipped this man, revered his swagger and unbridled confidence. Now, looking down on the sleeping, formless giant, he thought: No more of *that*.

"You know," he said softly, "I was going to ask for money—seeing as you have so much of it—but I think I'll just go ahead and take it."

Chin on chest, Burke slept.

"You'd do the same thing in my situation, wouldn't you? Take the money and run?" The shaved head was so shiny, so smooth and unrepentant, he had to touch it. "Or maybe you'd cut my throat, too, just to be on the safe side."

At this point Walt came in, carrying a cigar box. Vibrations from his Frankenstein-sized boots rumbled the floorboards, but failed to wake Burke. Then he stopped, seeing Parker on his knees beside the old man, gently rubbing his head.

"What's going on? Who're you talking to?"

"Gimme that." Parker seized the cigar box. He took out a Cubano cigar and lit it with a butane lighter packed inside. A bittersweet aroma filled the den and *this* roused Burke from sleep. He blinked at Parker, puffing away on one of his prized cigars.

"Didn't I tell you to get the hell out of Dodge?"

"Tomorrow, is what you said."

"That's right." Burke grinned. "We haven't had dessert yet."

The family in all its disparate parts gathered again in the dining room, enjoying coffee, vanilla ice cream and apple cider pie, Mother's specialty. Refreshed by his one-sided chat in the den and by the thought of the strongbox in the attic, Parker felt ample reason for hope. The luminous moon beckoned just beyond the French doors, an inviting terrain of moonlight and snow. One more time he looked across the table at Rita, attempting to convince her without words. *You don't have to understand. I'm taking care of it.* Smiling at Walt, he said, "What do you say we go to the lake?"

"What?" Walt spoke through a mouthful of half-masticated pie. "Who?"

He gestured at the three men around the table. "Us guys."

"You mean, *now*? What for?"

"Ice-fishing."

Burke looked surprised and delighted, as if someone had remembered his birthday. "Great idea!"

"But," Rita said, newly-alarmed, "it's late, isn't it? And cold out there?"

"We'll be fine," Parker assured her. He turned to Mother, anticipating protest. "Is that OK with you?"

Mother's gaze slid away from him and out the window. "Dress warm," she said.

"All right, men, let's get going." Burke set his coffee cup down and consulted his watch. "We'll rendezvous outside at . . . twenty-two hundred hours."

Walt seemed to regard the table and everyone around it from within a heavy fog. Rita was picking up plates, moving toward the kitchen. I'm on my own here, he thought.

"Let's go, men! On the double!"

17

Walt caught up with him in the living room, clusters of pie crumbs stuck to the corners of his mouth. "What's going on? Are you really leaving? What about Rita?"

"Things have changed—"

"No—not you! She's going with *me*."

His distress had a soothing effect on Parker. "First things first," he said. "We have strict orders to load the truck."

"That's another thing. How come you want to go ice-fishing anyhow?"

"Think about it, Walt. Just take a minute and think."

He gave it a shot—his brow furrowed, chapped lips pursed—emerging a moment later with an expression that might charitably have passed for cunning. "Yeah, OK. We could do something with that."

Eugenia appeared, in a blue-striped flannel nightgown. She'd run a brush through her thin white hair. Little sunspots of rouge dotted her cheeks.

"Did I hear someone say ice-fishing? Let's go."

Walt laughed nervously. "You can't go."

"Why not, Waldo?"

"*Walt,* goddamn it, the name is—"

"Waldo's right," Parker said. "It's much too cold out there. What about the Ice King? Where do you think he is?"

"On the lake. Where else would he be?"

"All right . . ." He eased her into the wing chair, to the accompanying symphony of her creaking bones. "Besides, someone has to stay here and listen."

"Listen?"

"To the house," he said. "Someone has to stay and hear what it says."

Relief at being finally understood flooded the old woman's face. On some level, he thought, we're perfect for each other. She lapsed into a coma-state, and for the first time since coming home, he felt to be truly in command.

The grandfather clock chimed in the dining room. Embers in the fireplace glowed like tiny insect eyes.

Upstairs, dressing in the dark, with each layer of clothing added, an opposing emotional burden—guilt, doubt, remorse—falling away. Time for a fresh start, and this time get it right. In this frame of mind he looked out the window and saw Walt lumbering through the snow, a crowbar in his hand. An odd sight, though by now that was almost routine.

A breeze rushed in from the open door behind him.

"It's true," Rita said, in the doorway. "You really are leaving."

He didn't know what to confirm or deny; all that was real

to him was touching her in the candle-light, the strawberry taste of her lips. Rita was no longer his sister or half-sister, or anyone but a girl he wanted to live out the rest of his days with, Polynesian-style.

"Is that why we almost . . . because you knew you were leaving?"

"No." But what he said didn't matter, he could feel a new prickly sensation in his head, like fingers sinking into moist pliable brain tissue, and realized: She's here with me.

You could still stop this. You could if you wanted to.

That's just it. I don't.

Halfway through the kitchen he noticed Mother sitting at the breakfast table in the dark.

"Well," he said. "We're off."

Her outline was visible, as well as the bottle and glass in front of her. "The facts, is that it? Is that what you want?"

"What?"

"So many things," she said. "His long nose, his funny little ears. And his weight! In all the time I knew him your father weighed exactly one hundred and sixty-three pounds, never more, never less. He could eat everything in sight and it didn't make a difference. When we went out to eat he'd finish his dinner and my dinner, then politely ask the couple in the next booth if he could finish *their* dinner, too. And still he weighed one hundred and sixty-three pounds the day he died."

It was too late for facts; Parker, sealed inside snow pants, two layers of sweaters and Walt's black pea coat, wanted only to get away.

"We may be out late," he said. "Don't wait up."

"Wait up?" She seemed startled, then amused by the suggestion. "No, I won't wait up."

Scolding winds hindered his journey from the house to the pickup, and when he got there it was empty. He watched his breath trail in vapors into a star-clogged night, thinking about the strongbox, the brain-addled memoirs, but mostly the money. *The future looms before you like an infinitely bright horizon.*

A steely hand clamped down on his shoulder, spun him around.

"Hey," Walt said, red-faced and excited, bundled up in hunting jacket, unlaced boots and mismatched gardening gloves. "Come on. I wanna show you something."

Tracing a path into the forest, they came to a clump of cedar and underlying brush. The snow thinned out and the ground was hard. Walt pointed toward a frost hollow a short distance away. "There," he said. Something lay half-buried in snow. Drawing close, Parker saw bloodstained fur, stiff twisted hindquarters, a tongue drooping from a fractured jaw. Ajax, in a pool of congealing guts. Beside him, tossed casually in underbrush, lay the crowbar.

"Didn't take but one swipe," Walt said. "You're right what you said—out on the lake's perfect. First chance we get, we drop the old man with the spud."

"The what?"

"Ice chisel. One good swipe oughta do it."

He took a last look at the old dog's remains, unwilling or unable to call up anger or grief. Things were sorting themselves out and there was nothing happy or sad about it. He turned back, heading for home.

"Hey! Wait for me!"

Walt climbed in the bed of the truck and took the gear Parker handed up to him—ice rods, bait bucket, tackle-box. Burke arrived to supervise in black flight jacket and a knitted cap with flaps over the ears.

"Ready, men?"

Turning, he whistled toward the tree line—a quick high-low sound that raised tiny hairs on the back of Parker's neck. There was no response.

"Old boy must be off chasing squirrels. Too bad. He likes going to the lake."

Walt jumped down and slid in behind the wheel. Parker held the door open for his stepfather, smiling a little too hard, like a mildly unbalanced doorman.

"After you."

They drove several miles on blacktop, headlights flitting across discarded farm implements, dozing cattle, a tractor-shed or two, before cruising on into rural darkness. Walt veered onto a gravel path that served as a secondary road in summer, cluttered now with icy potholes.

"Rapture," Burke said, seated comfortably in the middle, "how else to describe it? And best of all, ice-fishing at night! That giddy sense of release when the temperature drops—the *elements,* son. That's what draws a man forth from the comfort of his homestead."

Parker, sheltered from the elements by his own dark thoughts, barely heard. Ending a life—how hard could it be? Afterward, inventing a simple story: there was an accident, the ice wasn't as thick as we thought, Burke fell and drowned in the freezing water. Things like this happened all the time to people who'd done nothing wrong their entire lives. If anyone ever had it coming, it was Burke.

"I remember a winter night," he said, "many years ago. I was alone on the lake, crouched over the fishing hole, when a snowstorm struck. An enormous white wave coming at me from the east. Amazing sight—hypnotizing! Instantly everything went white, wind and snow in my eyes, my nose, my lungs—inside all of me." He sighed. "I was lucky. The storm passed. But for a moment that was the whole damn world, then and there."

Headlights splashed over barren oak trees.

"Rapture."

Trees parted abruptly. The pickup clattered to a halt at the edge of Ghost Lake, a broad expanse of flat pinkish ice ranging off toward darkened hillsides, a few cabin lights burning against blanket darkness. The smell of wood-smoke seemed very far away.

Parker left the truck, feeling edgy. Walt was already in back, gathering gear in his bulky arms and dropping it on the ground. He was edgy, too. "Hand back that lantern," he said. "Needs fuel." Pouring kerosene in the lamp's translucent casing, he kept an eye on Burke where he stood on shore surveying the scene, just out of earshot. "OK, soon as we get out there and he's not look—*damn!*" He'd poured too fast; kerosene spilled over the top of the wick tube, sloshing on greasy rags and months-old newspapers, washing across corrugated metal. Walt flung the empty can aside.

When they were ready, Burke led them along the shore past rocks and stumps, a weed-bed encased in ice. He paused at what seemed an arbitrary spot and—showing no doubt it would support his two-hundred-plus pounds—stepped on to the lake. He walked ten yards and then brought the ice-chisel's wedged blade down on the ice. An echo pounded to the sky.

"Any pike dozing nearby, that'll wake them. They spook easy but once we get our holes dug, they'll want to know what's going on. Pike are like that," he said, "real curious about things."

Parker watched him head out on the ice, lantern in his hand swinging like a beacon in fog. The time of night, the deep cold, the strangeness of this place, all worked against him; he hoped the old man would keep on going, until he was swept up in one of his goddamn mythical snowstorms.

Rough hands shoved him from behind. "Get moving."

"Maybe," he said, "there's another way."

"What?" Walt's eyes bulged behind his glasses. "Ain't no other way. Get moving."

Parker's first step was hesitant; he'd long since forgotten the sensation of frozen water under his feet. But the ice held and he was able to skid across, without grace but some velocity, shunning thoughts of the dark water below. Up ahead, the lantern placed on the ice cast a tricky light under the glaring moon, blocking everything else out. When he arrived at the chosen spot, the shoreline was just an abstraction, Walt's pickup invisible against the blank darkness of trees.

Burke knelt close to the lantern, inspecting the contents of the tackle-box. "Sometimes when I'm out here by myself, I put tip-ups close to shore, where bluegill tend to congregate. That way I can keep an eye on them from where I'm sitting." He rummaged through hooks, needle-nose pliers, rolls of fishing line. "Tonight feels more like perch, or maybe bullhead."

He looked down at his stepfather on his knees, then up at Walt. Now? Do we do it now? But Walt took the spud and began chopping, a brisk up-and-down carving motion performed with both feet planted squarely on the ice.

"See how easy it is, son? Just do like Walt, make your hole ten to twelve inches in diameter. Be sure to hold tight on the handle or you could lose it in the water."

"I believe I can chop a hole in the ice."

"We'll see."

Following their example he used the steel-chipped spud on the ice; each successive cut caused a quivering underfoot and he realized with a lurch in his stomach that the thickness of the ice was patchy at best.

"Are you sure about this spot?"

No one answered.

Sure enough, Burke's fishing hole was clean and well-constructed, in sharp contrast to his own gouged-out version. Burke leaned over the hole with a skimmer, clearing away chunks of ice. Again he tried catching Walt's eye. Well? What are we waiting for?

"No tip-ups tonight, son, but if you like, I can sound the waters for you."

He understood: Walt was waiting for him. "Sure."

Burke lowered a small lead-weight sounder in the hole, gently feeding out monofilament line through his gloved fingers. "Hmmm . . . I'd say six, seven feet. Just right."

Now was the time—while the old man's childlike joy at sounding the lake left him vulnerable and exposed. Parker threw his shoulders back, hoisting the spud upward as high as his padded limbs would allow. But the sharp motion acquired a life of its own, and he skidded backwards, a victim of blind momentum, the others turning in time to see him trip, slide and land hard on his face.

"Careful," Burke said. "Ice can get pretty slick."

He sat up, rubbing his jaw. Incredibly, Walt was laughing.

Soon three holes were dug and cleaned, three rickety stools placed a few feet apart in a semi-circle. Parker huddled close to the kerosene lamp, warming fresh bruises on his face. There was no comfort for his dignity.

"Cold?" Burke asked, holding out a thermos. "Try this."

The liquid, whatever it was, tasted like a blend of cotton candy and battery acid.

"Old Russian recipe—one hundred-sixty proof vodka sweetened with honey."

He coughed, trying to hold it down. It was just the thing. " . . . Thanks."

Burke took one of the ice rods, started rigging leader through a line-holder on the graphite grip. "All in the feel of the line, son. Perch like to sneak up, grab your bait like *that*—" He snapped his fingers, a muffled sound inside the pigskin gloves. "—then dash off to chow down in safer water. Pike on the other hand are quick-gulpers. If you miss the strike, you miss it all."

Walt fumbled and cursed, his fingers too stubby for the same delicate task.

"No, no, not like that," Burke said, reaching for the ice rod, "you're missing all the guides . . ."

"Leave me be." Walt held on. "I can do it."

The sight of them fussing over the ice rod made him laugh, even though he understood that, at bottom, he didn't know what was going on. Another long pull on the vodka-and-honey concoction, and he forgot what was so funny in the first place.

"Here," he said, extending the ice rod in his hands, "do this one."

"Gladly." Burke set about threading the line. "As for bait, we've got grubs, shiners, salmon eggs, whole-kernel corn. I advise shiners, myself. They don't get sluggish in low temperatures the way grub do."

"Whatever you say."

Using a dip net, Burke scooped a minnow from the depths of the bait bucket and held it up for viewing in the palm of his glove. Parker looked at the silver-scaled minnow, shocked to find himself suddenly locked in eye-contact with it, a desperate gaze across species, helpless to argue its fate. Then Burke plunged a sharp hook first through one eye, then the other; the minnow wriggled briefly and went limp.

The ice rods were all baited, hooks and sinkers dropped in respective holes. The grip in his hands trembled as the line met underwater currents of varying force. Time passed. They were ice-fishing.

"Splendid night," Burke declared, "millions of stars, not a cloud in the sky. I recall many nights like this behind enemy lines."

Parker, crouched tight against the bitter wind, silently cursed him. Fuck enemy lines.

"Hard to believe, but at one time in my life I dropped to earth on nights like this—blind drops mostly, where you never knew if the ground fires you were aiming for belonged to your partisan buddies or roaming *Einsatzgruppen.*" He paused. "Yugoslavia, is what I'm talking about."

Parker nodded.

"OSS."

And in the vaguely summer-theatre glow of the kerosene lamp, Burke described the sensation of free-falling on a starless Eastern European night, leaping from the plane at three thousand feet into mile-and-a-half winds, all sound ripped from your ears until the soft rustle of silk as the parachute opened and you drifted down into what you hoped was one small friendly patch of earth.

"Those were the days," Burke concluded.

A hush overtook Ghost Lake. Looking up, Parker imagined wave upon wave of fledgling spies falling from the sky. He noticed Burke fumbling inside his flight jacket as if scratching an obscure itch, and thought: I can't take much more of this. But when the old man squirmed free of the jacket and Parker saw what he was holding—the revolver from the desk drawer with an eagle on the ivory grip—he felt not alarmed so much as simply in thrall to the rush of oncoming events.

A long moment later, Walt glanced up from the hole; his eyes went to slits, the look of a cornered animal shining within.

"Easy now," Burke said. "Just go on with what you're doing."

Along with this thrill for events came startling new powers of perception; he could see delicate stitching in Burke's glove, the harlequin dance of lamp-light on the gun-barrel and, looking up, the pockmarked skin of the moon. As water slapped rhythmically at the underside of the ice, he reflected on the way in which things came to pass—things desired, things unintended. He shivered.

"Have some more," Burke said, handing him the thermos. "Warm you right up."

He drank, sensing Walt getting tight on the stool beside him. Burke sensed it, too, and trained the weapon on him. "Easy . . ."

Walt sat quietly. Parker smiled through numb, puffy lips, still hoping this was some bizarre joke. "You'll never get away with this."

Burke's laugh escaped in gusts of white vapor. "If anyone asks, I'll say we were set upon by poachers. A band of vicious Canucks robbed us at gunpoint, there was a struggle, shots were fired." More laughter in the face of Parker's disbelief. "All we have for sheriff is a flabby ex-truck farmer. I can make up any story I want."

Deputy sheriff. Almost a member of the family.

"What about you?" Burke demanded of Walt, who recoiled on the stool. "What do you have to say for yourself?"

Walt shook his head, as though he hadn't heard.

"*Well?*"

"I, I—I know what I see. I see you holding that fancy .45 you got in the war and I think maybe—"

Burke's smile darkened. "Patton."

"Huh?"

"This single-action Colt Army revolver belonged originally to General George S. Patton."

Either the information held no meaning for him, or Walt couldn't grasp its immediate significance; he stared at the gun and said nothing. Parker meanwhile schemed in a frenzy, though with the ice rod in his hands he felt helpless, almost too cold to move. Keep talking, he thought. There's always a chance if you keep talking. But all he came up with was: "It's not what you think."

Burke stood, extending his arms in a grand stretching motion, taking in a deep gulp of frigid air just for the hell of it. Removing his knit cap and sighing pleasurably as night winds raced across his scalp. *The elements.*

"Boys, I'd have to have been out walking on the moon not to see the intrigue brewing around here lately—eavesdropping, breaking and entering, ransacking personal papers. My house is overrun with thieves and hooligans and you don't think I noticed?" His voice echoed across the broad flat lake. "Years of retirement haven't dulled *this* old boy's seasoned antennae!"

"His idea," Walt said, choking back a frightened sob and pointing at Parker. "He found out about the money and made me go along."

Burke looked rueful in the flickering light. "Son, is this true?"

True? Not true? Who can tell anymore? "It's one interpretation," he said.

"I smell murder in the air," his stepfather announced. "For all I know, you shoot heroin in your veins and worship the devil."

"Well, I can deny *that*."

Still Burke's laser focus remained on the problem child. "They flushed you out of hiding, didn't they? Some cathouse in Nogales or camped out in the New York City subway system. Admit it! They'll do anything to keep me from writing the book."

"Who's *they*?" he cried. "Tell us who *they* is." And turning to Walt, freaked out anyway by the shouting and gunplay. "It's bullshit, just ancient Cold War bullshit—"

"Hey," Walt said, "don't piss him off."

"I don't mind. Young Parker here has what's known as 'an opposing point of view.' A revisionist, don't you know, forever remaking history in his own image . . . like a god. Is that it, son? Do you feel like a god?"

Raw winds pierced his clothing, freezing his blood. "Not at the moment."

"People like you," Burke sneered, "your *ilk*. You infect. You fester. You've brought to what's left of this century a very bad stink."

Cold, shaken, fearful of the gun, Parker didn't speak.

"Remember, son, I've been out there. I know what lies ahead." The old man started pacing across the ice, in and out of the fringed lantern-light. "I can tell you two things. One—when it comes it'll look like nothing we've seen before. Two—it won't end happy. Famine! Disease! Nuclear winter!" Baying at the stars like a drunken sailor. "Germ warfare! Jihads and acid rain!"

A flock of Canada geese overhead honked like cars stuck in traffic. Shifting his stance, Burke brought the combat-tested firearm to bear on Walt's horrorstruck face. "I mean to spare you all that," he said calmly. "It's nothing you want to be part of."

Walt made a gurgling sound, the shock of dying in his throat. Parker guessed the distance between him and the old man to be no more than four or five feet; he had to jump, he had no choice. Bracing his boots on the ice, he started to rise from the stool. Suddenly the ice rod lurched in his gloved hands—once, twice—causing him to look down stupidly at the hole. A tug on the line, and another. He had a bite.

Burke saw it, too, inching closer to the action. "Looks like perch," he whispered, "feed out some line but for God's sake don't spook him . . ."

No time to think, leader was spinning off the reel. As he yanked back, something electric coursed up his arms and through his body, in his mind a fish-eye's view of the underwater drama—perch takes shiners on its midnight run, hook snags fish flesh, a mad dorsal seizure and race for darker waters. Only the strength in his two arms holding it back. Parker held it back.

"Now! Strike him!"

The fish bolted one last time, taking nearly all the line, then went abruptly slack. He reeled in, thrilled in spite of himself.

"Easy, don't lose him—"

"I *won't* . . ."

A gawking fish-head emerged from the hole and then the entire perch—white-bellied, glittering red-and-silver scales, a good five pounds or more—lay flapping on the ice. He scooped it up proudly, displaying the fish for all to see in the lantern's yellow glow.

"Not bad for my first time, huh?"

It seemed in the next moment that Walt and Burke rose together and began dancing a happy fisherman's jig. There was shouting or laughter, in the burrowing wind he couldn't tell which. Something flashed by his face and thumped Burke in the chest. The gun twirled from his hand, sliding across the ice with the ice chisel. Walt's roar, as he leaped forward, cut through the wind.

The impact of crashing bodies toppled the lantern, sent shudders through the ice. Parker, still holding the fish, looked down at the jumble of arms and legs and felt a savage crunch underfoot. Seconds passed before he realized Walt was shouting at him.

"—gun, get the—"

Somehow, even pinned beneath the angry weight of one son, Burke managed to incline his head and gaze up at the other, as if to say, Is this the thanks I get? His free hand closed on the leg of an up-ended stool. Rolling sideways, he swung the stool in the air and smashed it into Walt's windpipe. Nightbirds squawked, disturbed by all the noise. Parker dropped the fish.

Walt sank to his knees, clutching his throat, sucking air in huge worthless gulps. His glasses tumbled into a hole in the ice. The old man slowly came to his feet, rubbing his eyes like a baby after a nap. In that moment Parker found the strength he'd been looking for, maybe all his life. Pushing off the stool he caught both of them in his downward spiral.

This time a low cavernous rumble swept through the lake, glacial water drenching their clothes as they grappled over the splintering ice. Now Parker was the one trapped under the men's combined weight. A hand seized his coat collar, pulled him free of the grunting mess—Walt, squinting at him and breathing hard.

"Look—don't—it's me—"

Just enough time to wonder if Walt knew what he was doing; then his fist caught a soft spot under Parker's jaw and dropped him on the ice. His head struck the rim of the metal tackle box. He closed his eyes and listened to angry subterranean rumblings, nothing human, the music of fish.

Moments later he sat up, tasting blood. His head hurt, but a sharper pain drew his attention to the fish-hook impaled in the fleshy heel of his hand. Beyond the toppled lantern, two figures were visible, one spread-eagled on ice, the other crouched overhead in an oddly intimate pose, like a hospital visit or deathbed confession. Peering closer, he saw that the kneeling figure had a grip on the other one's ears, was using them in fact to ram his head repeatedly against the jagged surface. Each time the victim twitched and gasped.

Parker tried standing, but pain kept him down. In a daze he watched the lifeless figure being dragged to a large hole in the ice. When the pummeled head came in contact with freezing water, there was a final orgy of physical resistance—bubbling screams, hands clawing at air—and the body froze in place, spine-bent and headless.

Once again the old man rose, a fresh wound over his eye, splotches of blood on his brush pants. Weaving through debris on his way toward Parker.

"Son, what say we let bygones be bygones?"

Fine by me, he thought. The gun lay on the ice a short distance away. Forcing himself up and moving through a dense fog of pain, he started for it and slipped, his boots going out from under him, and landed on his chin, shock-waves rattling his teeth. He thought he might pass out again—but the gun was in his hand. He rolled on his back and pointed upward, at pinwheeling constellations and the white-hot moon, at the descent of the man with a mad clown's smile and blood in his eye. He touched the trigger very gently at first, felt its subtle, insistent pressure. Squeezing, he thought: There's no place like home.

18

Hours passed, no way of telling how long. Gradually a new range of sounds filled the ice—crunching ice floes, a hawk's plummeting cry—and light rising in the east took on a sickly hue, the color of soured milk.

He sat up trembling, soaked to the bone, the surface around him littered with overturned buckets and minnows flopping on the ice alongside other unnamable bait. He had no idea where he was, no clear notion of what occurred last night. His fingers touched the back of his head and came away with dried blood and matted hair. Blood in his pierced hand had frozen solid. How long have I been out? Then: Where's my fish?

Two figures rested on the ice—still in the dream, he decided, just like I was. First to wake from the dream wins. This logic compelled him to his shaky knees and across the cracked, slippery ice to where one man lay stretched out in a blood-stained flight jacket, an arm shielding his face as if from the bright lights of heaven. Parker averted his own gaze as he bent and lifted under both arms, dragging the heavy figure to a serrated rift in the ice. Exhausting work, though a slight shove was all it took to guide him into dark, hungry waters.

The other man took less effort, sliding in the water and sinking quickly from view. A moment later, it bobbed again to the surface—slack-jawed, open-eyed, staring up at him. *I built that engine myself! Who else you know ever did that?*

"No one," he said.

Then began a long painful journey, hopping between fissures in the ice, reviving bruises in parts of his body he couldn't account for. All shapes of ice underfoot, chunks as large as a sofa, small as a cat. Nearing shore he kept an eye out for any sign of human presence; there was nothing but the truck's metallic outline in the low-hanging fog. He coughed, shivered, felt sick to his stomach. But when he finally made landfall and found keys hanging from the ignition, he knew his luck had changed.

The secondary road, flanked by spindly evergreens, went on longer than he remembered. Fog clasped the ground, making sharp turns harder to navigate. The pain in his head throbbed in rhythm with his injured hand, he was cold and hungry and tired enough, apparently, to doze off at one point, snapping awake just as the pickup ran a stop sign. Looming out of the fog was a moose—*the* moose, a legendary ten-point buck standing in the middle of the road. He swung left and for a split-second the truck lifted off the ground, or felt that way, before banging down hard again on two-lane blacktop. A desperate search in the rear-view mirror turned up empty: no moose in sight.

The fog had lifted by the time he arrived home. From behind the windshield he looked up at the old house—tall windows, pine-bright timber—wondering, What is this place? What am I doing here? He left the truck, walked by the towering rock elm and up the steps, hardly pausing to open the front door and step inside.

"Hey! Look who's here!"

Silence in the living room, kitchen and den. Upstairs, a glance in Rita's bedroom, and the others—all empty. Where was everyone hiding? In his own room he changed into dry clothes, stuffed belongings in a knapsack. She's got to be around somewhere, he thought. I'll find her, we'll leave. No discussion, just go.

But as he passed the study another thought occurred to him. Armed with a weak flashlight, he entered the attic, breathing dust, groping past boxes, drawn on his hands and knees to a particular cross-hatched beam in the corner of the rafters. Training the light over the side he saw the hinged aluminum strongbox, just as he'd left it, resting on a narrow plank between posts. He reached for the handle, grabbed hold and pulled.

Down the hall he felt a breeze coming from Eugenia's bedroom. Peering inside, he saw her asleep in the four-poster bed a few feet away from an open window. The room was as cold as a meat-locker.

"Eugenia, it's freezing in here."

She slept peacefully, blanket curled to her chin. In *her* dream, he suspected, she was greeting the Ice King. Something prompted him to tug the blanket away and check for signs of life. Her forehead felt as cold as the room itself—colder.

Memories came rushing back, the whistle of the spud flying past his face, ice cracking underfoot, a battered and beaten angel of death descending, a sound like fireworks, then a geyser sprouting cranium bits and red speckled pulp.

"I—I have to go now," he said, rising from the bed. "You keep on . . . sleeping."

Downstairs he placed the knapsack and strongbox by the front door, had one last look around. But the immaculate kitchen and the fire burning perpetually in the stone hearth in the living room had nothing to tell him. What's done is done, see what happens next. So thinking, he opened the front door and stepped into broad daylight, nearly colliding on the threshold with Leo Trunk, Ph.D.

A long moment passed before he gathered what remained of his senses.

When the door opened, Trunk was about to light his pipe. White gauze covered most of his nose, little strands trailing into his walrus mustache. As he struck a long-stemmed kitchen match, he took in the knapsack and strongbox and Parker's harried expression. He seemed to be in no hurry to speak.

"Look, if this is about the party . . ."

Trunk's eyes twinkled above the bandage. "Yes?"

"Well, uh . . . no hard feelings."

"You bet." The match in his hand still burned, despite the morning breeze; Parker was briefly transfixed by this tiny mystery. "Wind-resistant," Trunk explained, and lit the pipe.

Over his shoulder, a black BMW was parked on the road; there were suitcases piled in back, someone's shadow in the passenger seat. Surprise was making his head throb again. Fresh blood oozed from his impaled hand.

"Did you come for Walt? Too late, he's not here. Something

about flying to Easter Island."

"In fact, the island's aboriginal name is—"

"I know, I know."

"In any case, he won't get very far."

"Why not?"

"He can't fly."

"I thought you taught him."

"It wasn't for lack of trying." Trunk exhaled a cloud of cherry tobacco smoke. "And you? Are you running off as well?"

"Yeah," he said, staring at the Harvard professor's bandaged nose. "That's what I'm doing. I'm running off."

"It must be something in the air. Lately I've been thinking to hell with everything, time to pack it in. Thirty years chained to a classroom teaching the wisdom of the ages to one harebrained generation after another. Sooner or later you have to ask yourself, What's the point? Who profits from it, really? In the end, does any one of us ever learn from experience?"

His vision was blurred in watery patches, as if he was looking up through a hole in the ice. At the same time he had an answer to these questions, and took pride in sharing it now. "I do," he said. "I learn."

Trunk seemed sincerely glad to hear it. "Good for you."

"Well, then . . ." Lifting the strongbox, he walked the short path to the pickup. Trunk followed.

"What've you got in there?"

The strongbox landed with a satisfying thud in the passenger seat. "Family heirlooms," he said.

There was movement in the BMW. The door opened, a slender figure in a man's overcoat got out and walked through snow to the pickup. Early morning light sprinkled her shoulders, her face, her long black hair.

"We came back for a few things," Rita said.

"What the hell's going on?"

"A decision has been made," Trunk said.

He turned, a low growl in his throat—I've killed once, what makes you think I won't do it again? But Rita took a crumpled note from a coat pocket and thrust it in his hand, written in Mother's wobbly, tear-stained scrawl.

> *Alf and I have gone off in search of*
> *a ~~butter~~ better life. You should leave*
> *too while you've still got the chance.*
> *~~Gob~~ God bless.*

"She's right," Rita said. "It's time to leave the nest."

"No," he said. "Not like this."

"I'm going to Boston with Leo. He'll help me find a dance company there."

Trunk, slouched against the side of the truck, smiled as if to say, It's the least I can do.

"I knew it would be hard with you home," she said. "I thought I could manage it, keep us all together somehow . . ." She wiped away tears with the back of her glove. "I was wrong."

"Not like this. Not with this fucking guy."

Trunk laughed. "'Guy'?"

"Leave with me now," he said. "It has to be now."

For a moment he thought he'd persuaded her, but nothing glowed in her eyes and he knew he had lost. Like that moment back on the ice, when the old man raised the gun from his flight jacket. It was all going to happen anyway.

A crow settled in the rock elm's uppermost branches. The air smelled of pine cones and axle grease.

Inside the pickup, a great shuddering wave broke over him, pain in his head and heart. In the rear-view mirror he saw Trunk guiding her to the side of the road, preparing to say goodbye. He started the engine, shifted to reverse. Backing out, he saw Trunk again in the mirror, saw the match he'd used to light his pipe casually flung upward, still burning as it described a tiny arc of red light that sailed across the mirror and fell from view in the bed of the truck.

A loud serpentine hiss filled the air.

In the moments that followed he had time to consider all the things that mattered, those known about, those yet to come. Fruit bats and walking canes. Wild horses. Mud turtles trapped inside walls. Loose fuel lines and rags soaked in kerosene. The pale, empty moon. Then the gas tank exploded and a sheet of flames enveloped the truck from bumper to hood. Parker never heard the explosion; he was thousands of nautical miles away aboard a flying clipper laden with ice in its hold and bound for the equator.

Fire illuminated the sky, crackling red-and-yellow carnival lights bathing the crow in the tree, the faces of the man and woman by the side of the road. Soon the breeze caught the flames and billowed them upward. Smoke curled around the second-floor window, where the old woman stood in her flannel nightgown, nose pressed to glass, having struggled out of bed to see what all the fuss was about.

www.ingramcontent.com/pod-product-compliance
Lightning Source LLC
LaVergne TN
LVHW091640100826
845152LV00006B/108/J